Alix GAUSSEL

Sex after sixty

A Novel

Translated from the French by **Martin Waldman**

9 782954 299747

Paris, beautiful, 69yrs, blonde, writer.

It's the first line of my ad in the personal column for *Le Nouvel Observateur*. It's much too long. Each word is important because of the cost. Commas are useless. Instead of the Paris region, I can use the department number for the city --75. Of course, this supposes that respondents will not cheat. At my age, I refuse to take the suburban train, the RER, at night. 75, however, allows me to save eight letters. It also sounds more with it. I am going to use 75 and try to limit my contacts to towns on the Metro lines.

« Beautiful » it is often said seems cold and detached. For Baudelaire, beauty was a "dream of cold stone" Pretty would be easier; my friends think I am pretty. A graceful oval face little touched by time that a smile illuminates, coupled with a rather slim figure, thanks to daily rations of shredded carrots, legs well formed by water aerobics, breasts.... I would rather speak of something else. I touch them from time to time to be sure they are still there. They are not what they were and they will never be again what they were...

« Blonde » it's a miracle. But white hairs are beginning to infiltrate here and there. Soon I will look like a powdered wigged Baroness of the 18th century.

69! It's the magic number (!). OK. That was last year. We women do have the right to subtract a few years; we are excused for this little exaggeration.

75 pretty 69yrs blde writer

Seeks companion cltvd sstve

4 soul/sex rltnshp pht

Look at the second line: Companion that seems down to earth and real, more faithful and loyal than the potentially frivolous "friend" Companion by your side in good times and bad. « Cultivated » « sensitive », these are the only possible terms, much better than the snobbish « highly educated » and miles better than the «prominent social and intellectual position » that implies a fat bank account. Thank God, I am financially independent. I have my retirement and my English tutoring. I do not need to be supported by anyone. So I will go with « cultivated » and « sensitive » even if he is self-taught and even if he does not have any money. Money is not that important, what is important is a life well lived.

I keep thinking about all this so as to be ready to summarize on the telephone my seventy years in a few sentences in several minutes. I must be succinct and positive as well as thoughtful and graceful.

Two husbands, two sons and my books. Two children's books. Two novels. It is as if I want to contradict the old adage: Never two without three.

Yesterday, there was a phone call at four P.M. Because of the time, I correctly identified the caller as a phone solicitor. The young lady introduced herself and launched into her pitch:

- « You've won the couple's prize offered for the twentieth birthday of Bouygues Telecom. "You are part of a couple? »

- « No, not at all, » I reply.

- « I see... I'm sorry ».

She said as she hung up.

I have a lot of sympathy for these young people trapped in precarious jobs, but I do not appreciate being the object of their scorn. Doubtless, I am a bit bitter because I am not part of a couple. Still, I have adjusted rather well to my single state.

Last Saturday my friend Isabelle who I have not seen for quite a while came to lunch.

- « Anna, you do look good! How do you do it! ”

- « My husband left me.... » I jokingly explain.

We both laugh. It is partly true however. Since Jean-Pierre left I have lost eighteen pounds. I walk, I go to the pool with my daughter-in-law Laura, I am active. Last year, believing that I was going to die, I made a will. I took it to Counselor Cartier. I requested to be cremated and for my sons to scatter my ashes on the Seine from the Pont des Arts. I waited. Nothing happened.

My eighty-nine years old mother, still politically active in the polite circles of the far Right, invited me to stay with her in Bayonne, near Biarritz. I said « no thanks » and instead, joined the French League for Human Rights. I had thought about this for a while and was quite happy to have finally become a member.

Thanks to my computer I could go looking for Mr. Right on the Net like everyone else it seems. Today, no one is ashamed anymore about finding someone on the Internet. Personally, I think there are too many subscribers to various date clubs. This frightens me. Besides, I find the whole process time consuming. A printed ad in the personals column is more private. You get the letters at home; you have the time to study them. You can choose and only answer those that seem interesting. Of course, I realize that at my age many of my contemporaries do not have Internet.

The third line, speaking of « compatible in sensibility and sex » comes from my friend Isabelle. Following the thought, I bought new sheets, blankets and bed covers for my old bed. Since then, I feel like I am sleeping in the Château de Versailles. As for the photo request, I initially thought that to be too pushy. Still, I dreamed of a slim man with a helmet of white hair shining like a badge of courage.

I hand carried the ad to the offices of *Le Nouvel Observateur* because I feared my hand writing would not be clear. I wanted to read it together with someone from the review. Continuing my preparations, I made an appointment with Loïc, my hairdresser, for the following week. Just like the Girl Scouts, I will be prepared. My whole life I have always been prepared. Sometimes to the point that I infuriate my family and friends. I regard the time spent waiting for others as time wasted. Perhaps, not completely wasted because I can dream. I like to dream and do so except when a pupil is late for his or her appointment. Then I do not dream; I steam. I continue giving English lessons above all to practice my own English. I have three pupils: Valerie who is fifteen, Mohammed, eleven, and a twenty-two year old Pakistani whose name I always forget. My mother frequently reminds me that with the latter I should check the silver before he leaves at the end of the lesson. Obviously, I do not do what mother advises. I like speaking with him, he has a charming accent. He is a drama student who dreams of playing Hamlet. For him, it is Hamlet or nothing. This ambition does not prevent him from taking a summer part as a sword - carrier in his favorite play.

Who knows what I will do this summer? For the moment I have only one thought: the idea   that an envelope from *Le Nouvel Observateur*, full of hope, will be delivered Saturday.

The most curious of the letters I receive features a sketch in blue felt pen showing a couple making love. The man's head is hidden by the thighs of the woman. A few hand scribbled lines complete the charming communication. « There are lots of ways of having sex. The best is to have your very red lower lips licked. It's the best way to make a woman come ». Following the picture is the name and address of this inspired artist. The sketch is on tracing paper, obviously laboriously copied. The woman is smiling; just another lady in a bath smiling at the little fish coming to visit her. Curiosity makes me think I will call him.

Though sometimes some words are illegible, most of the letters I receive are carefully written and composed. Most are long. Most of the respondents flatter themselves. They are cultivated and sensitive to the highest degree to impress me. Several go so far as to cite Cicero and Lucretius, obviously authors that impressed them during their long ago school days. They range in age from 58 to 76. They live in a variety of places and exercise a variety of occupations. Different areas of France are represented with a large number of small city residents. One of the letters even comes from Marrakech in Morocco and another from Genoa in Italy. Some are deliberately teasing like Philippe who proudly affirms his antipathy toward literature and presumably writers. Another, a 75 year old architect with a sense of humor writes « I like your ad but I have a problem with the sex part. I am 6 ft. 7 inches tall and no normal bed suits me. Any suggestions? »

My formula «sensibility and sex » is a big hit. More so

than the personal description of the first line, my correspondents fix on this third line. I am a bit disappointed that so few creative people have answered my ad. Among the few there is a painter of the « New Italian Realist School", whatever that is. He sends me a photo taken in his Genovese studio. He is a handsome old man, really too old to play tortured artist.

One poet begins his letter:
Love comes on stage
No matter the age
Warms the head
And lights the bed

Among the more curious answers, I note a chess champion who has included a c. v. listing his many triumphs around the world. He is the only one who sends me a résumé fit for a job application. Changing tone, he includes a long poem called « Homage to the Beautiful Lady. » In it he asks if the Beautiful Lady is real or only a dream. He imaginatively continues with an « I see you as graceful and joyful, lively and spontaneous. » It is almost a declaration of infatuation. Unfortunately, there is no photo.

I look at the other snapshots. One shows a charming man dressed as if it was his First Communion. A pearl grey suit and white tie contain a thick featured heavy faced man. His letter is stiff and awkward. He is a 70 year old widow who golfs. He defines himself as an « organized person who lives a perfectly normal life. »What a nightmare! He admits to be twenty- two pounds overweight. Will anyone volunteer to make him loose them?

There is a photo of a 59 year old psychoanalyst who comes on like a guru. It is a computer generated picture above text sprinkled liberally with capital letters. « I am Emotionally Unattached and as I Was Touched by your

Advertisement I Decided to Write you and Answer you. » It goes on like that for paragraphs. He wishes to « Impart to you my Knowledge Concerning Human Nature » and he ends with a « Charming » self-portrait: « I am 5 ft. 11 inches and I weigh 225 pounds. If this Imposing Physical presence does not displease you, answer this Powerful and Protective Individual that a Woman can easily Become Attached to."

The following photo comes from Marrakech. It shows a tanned face capped by short curly white hair. Despite the deep wrinkles which mark the cheeks and forehead, it is a young face with a comforting smile, yet a certain sadness shadows his look. I have already nicknamed him "my roamer. «He writes me from a small hotel near Medina. He describes "nearby a square crenellated minaret lit from the inside. « The man is obviously in pain; his wife has just left him for a young tribesman. His sense of dignity prevents him from expressing his sorrow. Nevertheless, he says he is at peace, ready to welcome "whatever comes my way and whatever I find along the way." I am ready to meet him halfway but there are other photos which attract my attention. There is Daniel whose ruddy face and big smile more than second his claim to be a *bon vivant*. There is no place for nostalgia in his useful appearance. His letter is short. He is a business man who has no time to waste. He is a free man and is looking to share "laughs, hugs, tender moments and more if ...." He asks me to call after eight in the evening .Obviously; he has no time to lose.

Next, there is the photo of a country gentleman. A healthy outdoor look highlights his features. Under his bottle green sweater, his plaid shirt is tieless. He is a man of mystery; he likes detective stories and claims to know a secret that I must guess. He has the self-assured smile of a man confident in his attractiveness. I could very well see myself in his arms if he had not chosen to live thirty miles away from any urban conglomeration. Men like him are often quite lonely in the evening. Are they really attached to their loneliness or to their home?

I have a certain attraction for a gentleman in a brown corduroy suit who carries the fine name of Jean de Beaumont. His eye is lively, his forehead expressive, his hair rare. In all the photos I have still not found the helmet of white hair that I have dreamed about. Jean de Beaumont is an art historian who teaches at the Assas branch of the University of Paris. His raised engraved letterhead indicates the prestigious address, Avenue du Roule in Neuilly-sur-Seine.

All these desirable men await my telephone call. I have only to take the first little step and I can meet them. The headiness of power. I can give them all a trial in bed to see how they compare. Would I be able to tell the difference between Philippe and Daniel? Enough of dreams; stick to established procedures. Call those who are at the top of my list. Meet them in neutral territory, then have them over to my place. Stick to the advice that is given everywhere by everyone.

A dozen telephone calls later I have only spoken to answering machines. That is what happens when you call in the middle of the afternoon. Twelve times I leave the same message, "It is the blonde 69year old writer from *Le Nouvel Observateur*." That evening, I have the first reply.

"Hi, it is Michel."

Michel? Which one is Michel? I frenetically search the forty answers in my file.

I lamely ask, "Hue... can you tell me a little more, because...."

I am sure he is angry.

"Michel Destiens, I am a cardiologist."

I get it! The cardiologist! He sent me a sheet from his prescription pad on which he scribbled three undecipherable words. As if he thinks it enough to have an office on the Avenue de la Grande Armée to assure his success. Despite this, I agree to meet him. In the following days I make ten other appointments. Never in the same place. Often it is in the other's ballpark --a café in his neighborhood. I am curious to know the other's environment. If he has no suggestion to offer, I suggest two places appropriate for different circumstances. If they have the means, I propose the Brasserie Terminus Nord with its 1900 décor. For those less endowed, I offer La Maison Blanche, just around the corner from my place. For the moment, I am in charge. I have the power to decide, to choose, to propose. It is the only time I will have the upper hand. I use it. The chess champion has left me a message.

He has a nice voice, he invites me to dinner. He is the only one to do so. I have not yet succeeded in speaking to him.

Waking up the next day, I decide to wait for a call from José, the chess player. At 10 o'clock, my patience is rewarded. He has a deep voice, tinged by mockery

- "I would like to invite you to dinner, "he begins.

- "I would prefer to have dinner later. How about a cup of coffee near your office?"

- "But I don't have an office. I have a club. I have an idea, how about the Jardin du Luxembourg?

- "That's a good idea but the Luxembourg is very big. "

- "The chess players corner, just near the Orangerie of the French Senate, "he continues, "everyone knows where it is. Just ask. Let's say 5 in the afternoon. "

The problem is I already have two dates for the afternoon and the same for the day after. But can I say that? Each of these men thinks he is unique. They cannot conceive of competition from others.

- "OK, tomorrow afternoon, "agrees José", but afterwards, at 6 o'clock we will go eat at the Port du Salut Restaurant, in the rue des Fossés Saint Jacques…

Here is someone who has his own ideas and insists upon them. Power has changed hands. I feel obliged to accept his dinner invitation. These first contacts are like a tennis match. Or maybe like a chess match? I do not know anything about the latter, but I am willing to learn. Already, I realize that I am putting myself in risk in this balance of forces that is no longer in my favor.

Early in the afternoon I have a date with a certain "J.P" at the Aux Armes de Napoléon café near the Invalides. It is a nice day. I decide to walk there. I walk down the Faubourg Saint Denis, turn right onto the Quai de la Messagerie and continue on the Quai du Louvre until I come to La Passerelle des Arts. Under a changing sky the Seine is grey. A real Parisian sky, dotted with fluffy white clouds. I turn right on the Quai Malaquais, make a left on the Rue des Saints Pères and turn right at the Rue de Varenne. The golden dôme of the Invalides glitters in the distance. I have walked for almost an hour. Paris is small in the spring. The fine weather shortens distances and soothes the feet. As usual, I am early. It is a Café-Restaurant, its blue awnings snap in the breeze like flags. Inside I find a thick carpet and chairs that are too soft; the Viennese romantic music of the Beau Danube Bleu, present even in the toilets, begins to get on my nerves.

In his letter, J.P. calls himself a "Juvenile Prodigy" or a "Joyous Policeman". He is a high ranking civil servant in the Interior Ministry. Faithful to his profession he is watchful and suspicious. As soon as he sees me he leaps to his feet and leads me toward his table on the Restaurant side. Physically he is unimpressive. He looks like an old lady, with grey folds in his neck and a tic in his lower jaw. Unfortunately his name is not Jean Pierre, the name of my ex -husband as I believed, but Jules Planque and he lives in the neighborhood. On the Restaurant side the music is even louder. I suggest that we go outside for a stroll; J.P. sticks to his table and finishes his meal. I order a coffee.

He immediately begins talking and without pausing for a breath speaks of the opera by Debussy *Pélléas et Mélisande* that he saw last Saturday at the Bastille Opera, of the novel *La Douane de Mer* by Jean d'Ormesson, that he has just finished, and about an exhibit of 18th Century drawings that he recently admired at the Ecole des Beaux Arts. All this without a single pause. I get back at him with a low blow. I talk about the film of Pierre Bourdieu, Sociology is a Contact Sport, and the books of Pinçon Charlot on the wealthy neighborhoods of Paris. J.P. has a thin smile.

- "Extreme-left sociology?" He asks.

- "Certainly, "I answer with a certain aggressiveness.

This so refined cultural conversation and the Vienna Waltz music is unbearable. I have carelessly put myself in a nest of snobbery and arrogance. Once again I ask to take a walk. J.P. asks me to wait another ten minutes. I decide to be nasty and impolite.

- "I am astonished, I remark in my most honeyed voice, "that all these people put up with this music. They must have shit for brains...."

Although he is shot, J.P. does not stop smiling. He gives me a look and then without a word the Joyous Policeman surrenders. We leave for a walk. He says he will walk me to "my car".

- "No thanks, I prefer to walk. "

- Then without conscious of unconscious irony he concludes,

- "Well, till the next time. See you soon."

- "Yeah, real soon," I murmur while hurriedly leaving.

I walk back to my place via the Esplanade des Invalides, the Place de la Concorde, the Rue de Rivoli and Place Vendôme. I feel as if I am flying. When I get to the Place de l'Opéra, I think of taking the Metro. I am tired it is true, but I have not entirely ridden myself of the foul mood provoked by this "J.P." so I continue on foot going up the Rue Lafayette.

An hour later, I am sitting in the Maison Blanche Café, one of the centers of Western Civilization. Like the Perpignan railroad station was for Salvador Dali, the Maison Blanche will perhaps be for me the beginning of the end of my journey. It is an old café with a traditional décor, a bit smoke filled with waiters wearing black vests and the tables dressed in white. I am comfortable here. I sit at the outside terrace and order a Coca-Cola Lite. I await the arrival of "my roamer" from Marrakech; the one whose sad look so intrigued me. A historian, "an idealist, an aesthete, a man of many passions," is how he presented himself in his letter. Thirty minutes later I meet someone who collapses on the seat next to mine and does not even excuse himself for his tardiness. He has a very vague resemblance to his photo. The sudden departure of his wife with another has overwhelmed him. The wrinkles on his face are like slashes, he looks lost; there is no light behind his eyes. Everything he says is a long complaint constructed about the woman that he has just lost. It is impossible to surmount such an avalanche of bitterness. I let him speak for a long while and then I advise him to take his time and mourn decently before trying to enter into a new relationship. I then leave without a backward glance.

- "He is either going to drown himself in the Seine or he will recover, "I say to myself with a certain hardness, "but I will not let him take me with him."

I begin thinking with some apprehension of the two dates that I have to face tomorrow. There is Philippe, the architect who is too tall for my bed, and Patrice, the writer. I am sure that these two meetings are promising. But during the night I hear the slightly mocking voice of José remind me that we have a date the day after.

Philippe told me that he will be wearing a red parka when we made an appointment to meet at the Restaurant Antoine et Lili on the banks of the Saint Martin Canal. This young and inviting establishment sports a bright yellow front in contrast to the sober gray background of the bend in the Canal, near the Rue Bichat and the Villemain Garden. Philippe is there before me. It is easy to recognize him because of his height and his large sneaker clad feet. He does look too big for my bed. Blue eyed, friendly faced, he is physically acceptable; just as he wrote me. He had chosen the meeting place and immediately he goes to the heart of the subject. He chose this place because it is near the Saint Louis Hospital where he has a daily appointment since his kidney transplant. That is a major problem.

- "I am serving a suspended sentence, "he proudly proclaims before even ordering his meal, "my transplant is good for ten years, no more."

- "Your transplant? But cannot they give you another kidney? "

- "This my second one. They can't give me a third. The body is tired. I only have ten years to live."

He has put this huge matter before me as if he was giving me a gift. I am speechless.

- "Ten years are ten years, "I say with a certain distance as I try to console him.

Philippe does not answer. He launches himself in a medical explanation that sounds very often repeated. His transplant is three months old. He has not finished his transition period. He will be on medication for the rest of his life. All this he throws at me as if they were roses. It is his show. I wait until he has finished to toss back at him the question I've wanted to ask since he began.

- "Does your illness have an effect on your sex life?"

- "When you have renal insufficiency you are impotent, "he replies with an air of authority.

- "And you answer an ad that reads "soul and sex!"

- "You have to take chances. If I had not taken chances, I would have been dead long ago. But you are right. I am going to see a sex therapist."

- "That's a good idea. "

He opens his knapsack and takes out a first aid kit. He takes out a bottle, opens the cap with a practiced gesture, puts it in his mouth, and swallows the contents all the while looking me right in the eyes.

- "What are you doing? " I cry as I push myself away from the table, "it's disgusting! "

- "It's a medicine to prevent my body from rejecting my new kidney, "answers Philippe calmly." I have to take it three times a day."

- "I'm telling you right now I will not put up with that for ten years."

I try politely to look elsewhere. But I know that the medicine he should have taken before our meeting is still not finished.

- "You know," I say as soon as I can look at him again, "my friend Solange has a husband who got polio at thirty. He was not vaccinated. A year in intensive care, a year of rehab and then he goes home in a wheel chair."

Philippe nods to show he is listening and finally throws away his medicine bottle in the ashtray where I cannot miss seeing it.

- "Several times a day" I continue with a shudder, "he swallows his mucous. He has had a tracheotomy. There is a tube from an opening in his trash and it makes a scary gargling noise."

I add to the description an acting out: Both hands around my neck, my head shot back, my eyes bulging, my mouth open and making great sucking noises.

- "Solange put up with that for years. I couldn't have done that."

We say good bye a little later while promising to get together again. However, we both know that neither of us will do so.

At six o'clock I enter into the splendid Brasserie Terminus Nord, with its original Art Deco decoration. The chandeliers, and sconces, the columns, and the bar date from its construction in the 1920s. A young lady in a tuxedo guides me to a calm alcove. The waiters glide about in black jackets and white heavily starched shirts. I am waiting for Patrice Cornon, a writer who during our phone talk asked me many questions about our common calling. How did I meet my publisher? What percentage do I get on sales? How many copies of my latest were printed? How many review copies were sent? And on and on. I answered whatever he asked. I order a Kir and settle in to wait. Because I am always early for appointments, it feels like the other is very late. He does not show up. He was undoubtedly satisfied with the answers to his questions and does not think it is necessary to keep the appointment. I call him on my cell phone.

- "Mr. Cornon, please? "

- "The father or the son? "

- "Patrice Cornon."

- "He stepped out."

A slight hesitation in the voice warns me that it is a lie.

- "Please tell him for me that he is a pig."

I hang up, a bit comforted. Back at the house my answering machine has a message from Michel Destiens, the cardiologist from the Avenue de la Grande Armée. I call him back

- "Our rendez-vous is still on but I don't believe I told you that I am married," he says.

- "Why didn't you say that in your letter? "

- "It was up to you to state clearly that you were looking for someone without an attachment."

The last two days were full of problems. I am a bit discouraged. Fortunately, there is tomorrow's date at the Luxembourg Gardens.

To go to the Luxembourg Gardens I walk down the Boulevard de Sebastopol, cross the Seine using the Pont au Change and wave hello to the spires of Notre Dame. A pale sun gives a yellow tint to the buildings on the Quai de Montebello. I walk up the Rue Saint Jacques so as to avoid the crowds on the Boul'Miche and turn right onto the Rue Soufflot. When I come to the gates of the Garden I look at my watch and see that the walk took me 45 minutes. While it is true that I walk at a good pace, I am never bored walking in Paris.

Like Central Park in New York, the Luxembourg Gardens reserves under its chestnut trees a space specially for chess players. In front of the Orangerie of the French Senate, near the tennis courts, you will find, in good weather and bad, chess devotees. There are twenty odd tables featuring built in squares and scattered around on benches or balanced on chairs chess sets and players. They are neither rich nor poor, they are ordinary in appearance, they are chess players. Two young tennis players put down their rackets and pick up chess pieces. Behind them there is a group of old timers with gray hair and moustaches. The players all have a chess clock, a time piece with two faces, which counts the playtime allowed to each player. Everyone is fixed on their game. The feeling of competition is palpable. It is said that Karpov comes here to play for pleasure in his free time between two international matches. I wait near the old-timers table; it seems to me the place where the competition is fiercest. Suddenly I realize something which frightens me: there is not a woman in the crowd. Is chess a man's world? I look again at the mass of players and find to my relief, a woman; she has straight blond hair and seems thoroughly absorbed in her match. I return my attention to the old-timers table. It is up to my date to find me.

- "I will be wearing black, "I said to him," with a chain around my neck. Do not believe in the symbolism of either."

He laughed. I look up and he is there with a small smile on his lips and an air of authority in his stance. His eyes dance behind his delicate glasses. A fine head of white hair combed back completes the picture. He does not have to introduce himself; his face is the image of his voice. His eyes are green, his smile approving. Under his unbuttoned raincoat he is wearing a sea blue V-neck sweater. He is slim and elegant. And this full head of white hair is as unexpected as it is welcome to me.

He leads me to two empty chairs. We give ourselves over to the ritual exchange of information: family situation -- four sons and two ex-wives. He pays a fortune in child care and alimony.

"It's crazy," he says all the while smiling.

Divorced five years ago, he was looking to meet someone. By chance he picked up the *Nouvel Observateur.* He continues smiling as he tells me all this.

He begins to talk about the place and the players whom he knows quite well. The blond woman is a teacher who he has twice beaten. Most of the players are regulars. The game is not a spectacle and thus does not attract passers bye.

Answering a very precise question that I pose, he admits to be an International Grand Master. When I admit I do not know what that means, he simply adds that it is an honorary title awarded by the International Chess Federation to someone who has won a lot of matches. I would like to know more but José is not answering my questions because he is taken by the play on a near table. Our stay in the Gardens begins to seem quite long. The sun sets. At last we leave to go to Le Port du Salut Restaurant. I recall that the place was once a cabaret where I heard for the first time Anne Sylvestre sing Philomène. The piano is still there, arranged along the wall. They sit us at a corner table and I order a sole meunière. He has a strange way of ordering wine.

- "White wine," he unhelpfully orders.

My ex-husband studied deeply and interminably the wine list for the perfect inexpensive bottle.

José's life is made up of chess matches in all the major cities of the world. When he is in Paris he stays in a hotel; he will not tell me which one. He keeps looking at me with a mixture of admiration and mockery. The meal over, he has to leave me to play in a tournament at the Club du Chatelet. We walk there. As we are about to separate I suddenly raise myself on tiptoes and give him a kiss. He pulls back. I am smitten.

- "See you soon," he says as he disappears behind a door.

I carry away with me those three little words; see you soon, as well as the memory of his firm lips. Up until now I have had control of the situation. He has succeeded in taking away from me command, right from our first meeting. He is the one who decides, he is the one who is going to call me; I can do nothing but wait. Why then am I feeling happy? Am I still a young girl at my age?

The next morning, I am hard at work on the telephone canceling my other dates. It is quick work because I only talk to answering machines. I listen to the effeminate voice of Jean de Beaumont with some regret. Daniel's, the business man, call to mind his good humored pleasant face. It is hard, but I have to make choices.

I uncover the following number of *Le Nouvel Observateur*. I have neither the time nor the inclination to open the magazine and read my ad. I am swept up by the feeling that I must clear the way for the man I met last night. He did not promise me anything; he called himself a free man, looking for whomever he can find, and yet, I want to speed up the film of our future. So it is with a light heart that I eliminate the others.

As a member of The League of Human Rights, I have a regular correspondence with Michelle Tharp, an American sentenced to die for the murder of her seven year old daughter. Michelle has been living on death row in the Pennsylvania State Prison in Muncy for five years. She has been unwilling to talk about the circumstances of the act that led to her sentence. She has simply admitted to me that she feels terribly guilty. When I try to question her she refuses to answer. All that I know about the affair I learned through the Internet. Her little girl, Tausha, born quite prematurely, was afflicted with severe retardation. Was it because, as the prosecutor insisted, of abuse? Michele and her boyfriend, Douglas, found her dead one day in April 1998. They panicked and drove with the body to a nearby forest so as to hide the evidence. Then they went to the police to report her disappearance. Two years later, Michele received the death sentence. She is in a section with four other women also condemned to death. She and they are almost forgotten. I know almost nothing about the daily facts of their lives. Her letters tell me little. One day she let slip that two of her cellmates, in a violent outburst, covered the walls of their cell with their excrement. Michele and her roommate, Carolyn, who also has a correspondence with our group in The League, are forced to live under such conditions and even obliged to clean the walls when necessary. Michele is depressed and medicated heavily, yet she does not complain to me. She asks me about my life, my activities, and my children. She seems very interested in my opinion about America and often talks about how she does not like what Bush is doing. She speaks to me sometimes about her children, Tonia, Ashley, and little Douglas Jim. They are in a foster home. She sent me a photo of herself; A youngish blond of around 35 who seems a bit lost amidst her large family. Douglas, also in the picture, "who makes a fool of himself" by trying to make scary faces for the camera. Last Christmas I asked Michele if the children would visit her for the holiday. She did not answer my question. I later found out that the Christmas holiday was a very hard time for her. I understood then that she was unable to see them. The only distraction that Michele has is the mail. She has several "penpals" and is always looking for new ones everywhere in the world thanks to the Internet. It is this lifeline to the outside which keeps her going and stops her from completely disintegrating. Every time I write Michelle it is for both our benefit.

I struggle against the wish to call José. Finally, I have his mocking voice on the telephone. He says he will meet me on the Boulevard Saint Michel in a bar called Le Reflet right across the street from the Reflet Medicis movie theater. It is a secretive place; everything is painted black, including the floor and the tables. It is a meeting place for chess players and chess lovers. There are several in Paris. Here, you can find a partner for a match in less than five minutes. Loud jazz music fills the air. As usual, I am early. I take a table near the door and order a tomato juice. He comes in at exactly the time agreed upon. The smile is still there, the lips are still closed. His jacket floats on a skinny body. The eyes are those of a man who knows how to smile. He orders a coffee and goes to the rear of the bar with a chess board. We set up the pieces together, as I try to remember what I learned as a child. I last played chess... sixty years ago!

- "White starts and wins, "he says while turning the white side toward me.

I move the king's pawn. He does the same. I advance a knight. Then the second knight. Then I stop and admit my inability to go further.

- "It's the knight's offensive," he says.

- "Play for me"

Smiling all the while, he makes several mystifying moves and then declares that I have won. He lays down his king in admission of defeat.

- "Tell me about the history of chess," I say.

- "It all begins in the Fifth Century in India. A Wise Man named Sassi supposedly invented this game so as to make the king think about his kingdom. It is a war game. The chess pieces represent different actors in the battle. There was an elephant, cavalry, a war wagon and foot soldiers. The elephant became the bishop and the war wagon, the castle or the rook, the foot soldiers naturally became the pawns. The queen shows up much later, in Europe during the Eleventh Century. "

- "Is she the symbol of femininity? "

- "It's better than that. She is the most powerful piece of them all. She can move in any direction. Today we call her Madame. Maybe The French Revolution has something to do with the name change. Royalty is not well regarded by us. "

- "Chess," Jose continues, "is a reflexion of its time. In the beginning, dice were used, but Islam and Catholicism were against games of chance and above all gambling. As a result, the dice disappeared and chess became one of the few games where chance does not play a role."

A bit later, we say goodbye outside the bar. I am very careful not to repeat what I did last time. He seems satisfied to look at me with his bright eyes. I leave, taking with me the same three words, see you soon. All the others --the Philippes, the Daniels, the Michels, are forgotten. Yet, from time to time, I still look at their photos.

It is often said that the children of parents who are looking for a new partner are extremely hostile toward the newcomer. This is not the case with my sons. They have always supported me in my searches. My eldest, Lucien, was the one who advised me to take an ad in *Le Nouvel Observateur.* Ten years ago, he and his wife, Laura, met in such a way. They have never regretted their choice. My sons often ask me about my progress. Adam, my youngest, is likewise behind my efforts and would be pleased to have a new step-father. Both of them prefer to see me happy rather than always alone. However, I realize that I must not ask too much of them. They do not have to hear about my sex life. All the psychoanalysts tell us a mother is sexless for her children. Once they are born, their mother no longer requires or wishes to have a sex life. Lucien is shocked when I bring up the subject. A partner is fine as long as he keeps his distance and keeps his pants on.

This Friday, like every other week, I go to my memory workshop at the Emerald Club on the Boulevard Richard Lenoir. I join up there with twenty old, gray or white haired seniors, almost all of whom unfortunately are women. The workshop leader, Annick, leads us in two hours of speech and memory exercises. This workout seemed to me obligatory, when one day I could not remember the name of a street that I knew quite well because I worked very near it for years. I tried the Rue Vadim, the Rue Vabien; I could not remember the Rue Vavin. At that moment, I decided that I must fight back if I wished to avoid more frequent memory lapses. Since then, I make every effort to assure that proper names are not forgotten.

Upon my return from the workshop, I find a message from José. The day after tomorrow, the Channel beach resort Berville will hold the Eighth Annual Chess Tournament for Master Players organized by the local chess club and the International Chess Federation. Ten world class players will meet in this most well-known French Tournament.

These champions are all young; the eldest is only 34. There four Frenchmen, two of whom are international champions, will play against players from Russia, Armenia, Holland and Moldavia. The current trend is to find younger and younger players at the highest levels.

When José and I walk in to the municipal events center the first series of matches have just finished. There are small tables where the competitors are seated. High up on the wall behind them are individual screens which show the game board. In the shadows, there are three rows of bleachers almost entirely filled with spectators. José leads me to a free place. The players are very fixed on their game, as is the public. Complete silence is the rule. Not a cough, not a sneeze. I silently try to follow the undecipherable wall screens. Suddenly I feel José's hand on my thigh. I stop reading. The hand is self-assured and insistent. It begins to move up my thigh. Not for a moment do I think of stopping its progress. Any movement on my part can attract the attention of those sitting around me. It is also true, that I find the adventurous hand exciting. The hand arrives at my groin and stops. I hold my breath. And then José takes my hand and places it between his legs. There is nothing obscene about the gestures. They are rather signs of affection. I stay calm. I feel the heat of my blushing leave my face. I am a bit dizzy. For almost an hour, without moving, I feel his heat under my hand and his hand so intimate with me. I attempt to concentrate on the chess matches which play out in front of me. Finally, the last match is over. I dare now turn my head and look at José in the darkness. The president of the club announces that the prizes will be distributed in two hours. I am surprised that I manage to stand up. I am very thankful that José takes my hand and leads me to the exit. We walk towards the water. The sea is dotted by a fine rain. We walk along the boardwalk which is lit here and there by streetlights in the style of the 1900s. My hand is deep in his coat pocket. I feel his fingers about mine. At the end of the boardwalk there is a tearoom which welcomes us. We order an bergamot tea. The rains have stopped and the water has regained its calm. A wind sailor sets out.

The prize giving ceremony is touching. One by one these young champions come up to receive their trophies. Each of them takes the microphone to say how happy they are and to thank the public for their welcome. The mayor of Berville gives a speech. Afterwards, the children who are members of the club are honored. They range from 6 to 12; there are many girls among them. After the applause ends we go up to the buffct supper. I am proud to be with José; He knows everybody and introduces me to everyone. We say hello to the parents of the players. A journalist from *Echecs Magazine* who has covered the Tournament judges the play to have been of a high caliber.

When José and I separate, I am agreeably surprised to receive a quick kiss. The day was too exciting; it takes me a long time to fall asleep.

Several days later, when José telephones, he asks me if I will be free all day long in two days' time.

"It will be a hot day, "he says, and I sense a smile in his voice.

He shows up at ten. His eyes as always are shining and his voice is gently mocking when he looks at me. He come into the living room and casually undresses while inviting me to do the same. He is shameless and he is already erect. Not at all anxious, he takes me in these arms and leads me to the bedroom. It is like assisting in a sacred ritual. He has still not kissed me. He carefully lies me down on the bed and looks at me as if I am a treat that he will soon savor. He then turns and places on the night table a chess clock with two faces and hands. I am curious. Here I am lying on the bed, my legs stretched out, my shoulders back, waiting for what comes next. He sits down beside me, in the Lotus position, like a guru instructing a novice. With a confident hand, he separates my legs. He explores me with his tongue.

- "Delicious, "he says.

A moment later he stands up, presses the start button on the second chess clock and lying down beside me, makes clear that it is now my turn to play. Completely relaxed, I raise myself on an elbow. His penis is purple, with dozens of little veins scattered in all directions. I take it in my hand and then in my mouth. Like a little animal it answers my fondling. I play with him for a long time.

- "I adore your hearty appetite, "says José breathlessly.

He then gets up, goes into the living room and pulls out

a package of prophylactics. From his jackets pocket.

- "Chocolate flavored", he says with a huge smile.

While he casually rolls on the small rubber tube, I take the opportunity to look at him. I see his skinny arms and legs, his too pale skin, his ribs sticking out from his hollow stomach; but his shoulders are still straight and proud.

- "I feel so good inside you," says José as soon as he penetrates me.

His pleasure relaxes his face and smoothes the wrinkles from his forehead. He intensely looks at me. I respond to his every movement. I feel the spasms of my pleasure.

- "Can I shake you up a little?" He asks me after several minutes.

He then proceeds to give me large deep thrusts. He lets me rest for a moment before the next delicate operation. Turning on his back he maneuvers me on top of him; all the while resting joined together.

- "It's the small castling," he says as we find our positions reversed and my head is above his face.

I do not know anything about this small castling and I am a bit anxious about the possibility of a big castling. For the moment, at least, José puts his head on a pillow, leaves me, and takes a break. Soon after, he puts his elbow on the pillow; his head supported on his hand and begins to talk.

- "All chess players know the legendary masters and the tales of their exploits. Do you want me to talk about them? "

- "Of course."

"In the 18th century," he begins, "there was a genius named Philidor who completely changed the game. He used his pawns as no one had ever done before. 'Pawns are the heart and soul of chess, ' he said. At the time, France was the world leader in chess; but soon England would take over. It was the time of the glittering cafes: The Cafe de la Régence, The Place du Palais Royal. Everyone famous was there: Voltaire, Diderot, and Rousseau. Later there was Robespierre and Bonaparte.

"When London took over, the Englishman Staunton pushed his ambition to its limits. He challenged the Frenchman Saint Amant in France. When Staunton won, he proclaimed himself World Champion. Later, from the United States, a new star burst on the scene. It was Morphy who was called the Mozart of chess. At the age of ten he was already shown off by his parents who dragged him from club to club. He was always dressed like a little prince with velvet pants and a lace shirt. He beat everyone he faced and very quickly became champion.

Shortly after in Austria a new contender, Steinitz, came on the scene."

We hurriedly lunched on smoked salmon, chilled wine, and pears in chocolate sauce. Once our coffee finished, we undressed and went back to the bedroom. José began talking while making love. He picked up his story where he had left off, all the while containing his pleasure so as not to be interrupted in his actions and words.

- "The chess world was upside down. Steinitz' style shocked and scandalized his contemporaries. He set up his defenses and waited for the attack of his opponent. He thus exploited the errors of the opposition. Finally, a Pole, Lasker, won the World Championship. Steinitz faded away after thirty years of domination and became crazy. From his hospital bed he challenged God and gave the Deity a handicap of plus one point. He died shortly thereafter without ever regaining his lucidity.

"His tragic end shortly after the nervous breakdown suffered by Morphy, helps spread the idea that a passion for chess makes you crazy. This idea was picked up in imaginative literature. Stefan Zweig in *The Chess Player* and Vladimir Nabokov in *The Defense* offer us characters so thoroughly engaged in the game that they become insane. Later, in the United States, the life of the American champion, Bobby Fisher, a New York Jew whose flights of anger and depression were totally out of control, will serve to reinforce this hypothesis. "

"In Russia, they nurture chess and chess players. They have made it a national sport. They play everywhere, in schools and in factories. Women also play. Vera Menschik becomes the first female to win a World Championship. Everyone pays attention to the meteoric rise of Anatoli Karpov who becomes World Champion at 23. Then the Gorbatchev supporter Gary Kasparov takes away his title. We are now at the beginning of the era of chess champions as world famous stars. The two Ks for a long time were unbeatable. In France we are patient and we hope to see one of our young players become Champion."

While still talking, José hugs me tightly and says,

- "Now you are going to have the opportunity to have the Big Castling", he says tenderly.

Supporting himself with one arm he picks me up and stands up. I cooperate and circle my legs about his waist. Joined together we parade around the apartment. As soon as he spots a sign of pleasure on my face he puts me down on the bed. And then quite suddenly he collapses on his back. Not a word is said but I feel his body no longer answering mine. The inner strength which had pushed him forward is gone. A moment later, now, no longer talking, he retreats into himself and seems to withdraw in pain.

- "I think I did too much today," he finally says with a small voice.

Concerned, I try to cheer him up. It is no use. With a sigh he makes me understand that he is finished and he begins to collect his clothes. He refuses to look at me.

My chess champion left without saying goodbye. I imagine he is already thinking of the next tournament he is going to play in at the other side of the globe. I try to calm my fears but I am afraid I will never see him again. I did not hear those three dear words "see you soon", which would have been so welcome to me. I will call him several times in the coming weeks. He never called me back. I have nothing to remember him by; not even an address. He goes from chess club to chess club, from woman to woman, without forming any attachment. For me, he is now part of the legends of chess, like Philidor and Morphy.

I bought a chess board and I taught my grandson, Clément, how to play. He beats me all the time. I am not a good player. He is very proud to be able to play this grownup game.

I am not someone who wastes time hashing over my setbacks. After several days of healthy mourning, I reopen without bitterness the folder containing the letters of my potential suitors. The almost forgotten photos, the never opened envelopes that I have saved, are full of promise for the future. My determination is firm and hope is alive. Tomorrow, I will call Daniel and Jean de Beaumont. I open the few letters in the second batch sent by *The Nouvel Observateur.* I make a list of calls to make and I sleep on these new plans.

Every Tuesday, regardless of the weather, my daughter-in-law, Laura, and I go to the Jonquière swimming pool. With the pleasant May weather, it is very easy to walk to the pool. This is not the case during the winter when the wind blows harshly and the snow swirls about. When the weather is fierce, we do not find many others in the water. Today, with the sun shining through the glass roof, there are many new voices echoing in the showers.

Laura uses a graceful breast stroke which makes full use of her long legs. Every week she does twenty laps. She is a beautiful raven haired woman with a lovely neck, high cheekbones, elegant hands, and well-shaped legs. Every time I see her I think of how lucky my son was to have met her thanks to an ad in the personal columns. She was the only one who answered his ad. She has never disappointed him. After our swim we often lunch together in the pool snack bar. We talk about the children and her work as a supervisor in a luxury Parisian hotel. Despite the birth of her second son, she continues to work the taxing double shift which forces her to work one evening a week up to eleven at night and begin work again at eight the following morning. This leaves her a few hours of sleep. The double shift is a nightmare; it takes her the following two days to recover.

I am careful not to speak with her about my potential or actual love affairs; just as I avoid the subject with my sons. One time when I started to talk about it, she left the room. Since then, I respect her refusal, knowing as I do that she has to listen to her mother go on about the subject. Yet today, I really would have liked to ask her advice. She always offers wise counsel. Yesterday, Daniel, the business man, refused to start up again a contact that I had broken. He did not call me back. And Jean de Beaumont is starting to show signs of being a bit bizarre. He was only too happy to make a date to meet me but his voice was uncertain and his answers vague in response to questions that I asked him concerning his life and work. Likewise, he was evasive as to the University where he supposedly teaches. When I offered to meet him when he finished his last course of the day, he substituted the name of a café in the Latin Quarter as a place to meet. It seemed a bit incongruous for someone with an engraved letterhead bearing an address in Neuilly. Nevertheless, we met in the covered section of the Saint Séverin Café in the Place Saint Michel. I find before me a man, a bit overweight, with a round face and a carefully trimmed beard. He has an old-fashioned charm coupled with perfect manners. He asked to be forgiven for his lateness in a totally disarming way. However he does not at all seem like the person described in his letter. He smiles a lot but he is so shy that I do not see how he could teach a class. He shows off his cultivation by talking a lot about Baroque painting. In his large pockets there swim two or three copies of the sophisticated series "Découvertes "published by Gallimard. He listens only to classical music and owns, he boasts, two thousand CDs. He concludes by describing himself as a charming destitute intellectual living in the maid's quarters of his mother's apartment in Neuilly. He owes his splendid education to his English mother but she is also responsible for the emotional backwardness from which he suffers. A problem that he is looking to solve by meeting a woman of my age who will be his second mother. It is true that he is almost ten years younger than me. He tells me all this in a matter-of-fact way as if it is all perfectly normal and thus should be acceptable to me. He never stops smiling and talks much of all the exhibitions that he goes to every day. We are supposed to meet next week at the Louvre.

In the coming days, I am due to get to know Fabien, and Philippe Massier another Philippe. Fabien's letter written on blue paper begins by, "How, in response to your expansive epistle, can I force your attention to me? While I love words, it appears to me that in this context they are inadequate. I will soon be 69 years old, I am divorced and my two daughters lead their own lives. I am a book editor. I am physically acceptable. I am looking for a synergy of minds so as to form a lasting union that will be as uncomplicated as possible."

Here is a man who does not want complications. Seeing as he is a book editor I called him immediately. He called me back the same evening. A young voice that sounds sincere. We fixed a date and time for a meeting in the Boulevard Saint Michel. I chose the place, the Tea Caddy, a very British tea room where I often went with my mother to eat cinnamon toasts.

Philippe Massier's letter also showed curious personality; maybe a singular and interesting one. He is probably a mixture of bad boy and aging misanthrope. At least that is the impression I get from his note. It is the combination which is attractive. There is no photo. What he does, however, is describe at length his routine. The goldfish he chases; his working week-ends that he wishes to keep undisturbed; his messiness; his 65 years; his baldness; his MBA; the list of his qualities and activities is long. All this is quite acceptable to me, except for the week-ends. Is there a place for a woman in his life? Fortunately, there are these words, "but I always have time for things I love." When I call him, I hear an authoritative voice, with a slight drawl on the answering machine tell me.

- "You are speaking to Philippe Massier's machine."

Immediately, the machine asks me for the date and time

of my call. I have never encountered this before. I leave my name and number with a brief message. He calls back the next day. His voice is slow but sure. Once again, he lists how he spends his time, the routines that he does not wish to change, his studious weekends, and his full Mondays working to prepare his Tuesdays sitting as a judge at the Business Court. So he is a judge. He sits in judgment Tuesdays. Tuesday evening, he is exhausted but happy. He laughs, he sings, and although he does not say so, it is obvious, he screws. He lives in a small street near the Odeon Theater. I am a bit overwhelmed. Suddenly, he stops talking and asks, "What about you? Tell me about the last movie you saw?"

Now, it is my turn. It is sort of like a school exam. I have to provide an answer. Luckily, I know a lot about the subject.

- "I saw Pedro Almodovar's *Talk to her.* "

When he remains silent, I continue:

- "I did not really like his first film, *Women on the Verge of a Nervous Breakdown.* I found it too male chauvinist. But then there was *High Heels* and that is a fine film about women. However, I did not much like, *About My Mother* which was a big hit. As for *Talk to her,* it is a very brilliant and very moving film. Almodovar is a director who goes to the limit. He creates people who are extreme and about to explode. ..."

Out of breath, I finally stop. Silence at the other end of the line. I think he is impressed and respectful. He proposes a meeting but without specifying time or place. He will call me back in a few days. This man slips away all the time. Here is another example of the power game which takes place in woman-man relationships. I had the upper hand and he took command away from me. I am now supposed to be at his disposition. It is quite frustrating. And yet, fortunately, there are the words "for what I love."

It was at the Museum de la Vie Romantique and not at the Louvre that Jean de Beaumont and I met one morning in mid-May. We thought we would take advantage of a sunny day for a « lunch on the grass » in the little garden next to the brick house that was formally the home of the painter Ary Scheffer. Being polite, we admire together George Sand's water colors called « dendrites » named after the fossilized trees of her Nohant home. Afterwards, we went to the cafeteria, and seated under the protective canopy, I selected a zucchini pie while Jean opted for a lentil salad. I suspect he chose the lentils because they were inexpensive and I teased him about his miserliness. As soon as we were settled at the green shiny table behind several low bushes, the discussion took a more serious turn. I wanted to know where he teaches and if I can sit-in on one of his classes. After much hesitation and embarrassment, he decides finally to tell me the real story. He is not a teacher. He is like me a tutor for foreigners temporarily living in Paris. He never earned any degree because he has problems concentrating on his studies, he does however follow free courses at the Louvre where he learned something about Art History. He finds his students for French lessons with ads in *Fusac*, the periodical for English speaking foreigners living in Paris. The pocket money he earns allows him to go out occasionally. His parents do not live in Neuilly but rather somewhere in the South of France. His street address is however accurate; although he lives in a maid's room on the seventh floor without an elevator. To top off everything, he makes ends meet thanks to a check he gets from the Handicap Aid Program that he began receiving at age thirty-seven when he returned penniless from a trip to Vietnam. His psychological problems are real enough but he exaggerated them so as to get support. I don't know how he did it and I don't want to know. I am speechless. How could I be fooled so completely? Was I hypnotized by his aristocratic name?

- « And the letter head? » I ask.

- « Anybody can have stationary made. Moreover, my name is not Jean de Beaumont. That's my pen name. »

He then shows me a yellowing excerpt from the long disappeared review *Arts*, where he had succeeded in having accepted twenty years ago an article on Ingres that he wrote *when* he was auditor at the Ecole du Louvre. He then informs me that Beaumont is a commune in the Eure Department. He excuses himself for having fooled me but he insists that if he had told me at the beginning that he lived on a stipend from the Handicap Aid Program I would have never given him a look. He hopes that I am not mad at him and that I will be his friend, nothing more than his friend. I feel sorry for him and tell him that I will not drop him. He is so grateful that he suddenly gives me a big hug, kisses me on both cheeks, and immediately starts talking about plans for our next meeting. Carried away by his enthusiasm, he skips away making me promise to call him next week. I walk back home via Avenue Trudaine and the rue de Dunkerque. While it's true that advertisements are a most fertile ground for lies and exaggeration, the learning and openness of Jean is very real. Becoming friends I formed a link with him that I will not regret. Soon after he cast aside his pen name, his letter head and almost all his exaggerations and fabrications. However he will choose a girlfriend several years younger than me. He will then continue to see me, henceforth as a second mother to whom he can confide his romantic's secrets. I censure him when he drinks too much, I console him when he loses one of his students and I listen to all his silliness.

Despite the lies, the false trails, the setbacks and the disappointments, these men of the personal ad columns all offer me something. Some bring me knowledge, others information and others another way of looking at the world. When I make an effort to penetrate their universe it is the beginning of an adventure. It takes time, it involves moments of discouragement but I believe it's worth it. I meet different people of many interests, I win friends --even for a brief time -- and I gain experience of inestimable value. An extraordinary world opens before me for little money and many precautions. I have not stopped learning about human nature and I will have later in life lots to tell to my granddaughter Juliette who is now a year old, I am going to tell her that she must love men, because they are truly marvelous.

This morning an envelope postmarked Pennsylvania with a typewritten letter from Michelle arrived. She thus has had permission to use the library. I write and ask her what she had to do to win that. Her letter, always too short, is friendly and open. As always, she asks a lot of questions and does not answer mine. I am not displeased by that. I know only too well how hard her life must be. She tells me that every day is a struggle. There are many accounts of the condition of those on Death Row. The loneliness, the continual racket, and the awful smells. Michele has suffered all that for five years. In addition there are the problems she faces because she is a woman. A recent study done by the well-known American Civil Liberties Union talks about the especially difficult conditions under which women condemned to death must live. Presently they are fifty something, all from poor backgrounds. Because there are so few they are often completely alone. Fifteen of them are the only women on Death Row in the State of their conviction. They are thus completely isolated from the rest of the female prison population. In addition, most are abandoned by their family and do not have visitors. A third of the group complain about the salacious looks from the male prison guards when they wash up or change cloths. The ACLU calls them "the forgotten population." The execution of Karla Faye Tucker in 1998 lifted the fog of indifference a bit. The media found in her a young and pretty woman whose case sparked interest for a moment. Interest that soon declined although some women, like Priscilla Ford, live on Death Row for twenty years.

Saturday, I spend a special moment with my grandson Clément. While we are watching at a cassette of *Peter Pan* together he snuggles up in the crook of my arm and offers me the gift of his presence.

Fabien is the one whose letter on blue paper had a certain charm; although he wishes to have no complications. For me, who has not succeeded in getting a third novel published, his prime asset is that he is a book editor. When I walk into the Tea Caddy in the Rue Saint Julien le Pauvre, I go right towards a man sitting alone near the fireplace. As he had written me, he is acceptable looking. His gray hair is combed back, his nose a bit hooked, his clothes well cut. I sit down next to him so as to be warmed by the wood fire. It is a rainy afternoon; this month of May is fickle. I order an herb tea. Fabien is all smiles and attentive. He repeats the information contained in his letter. Although he is retired, he continues to edit books for his pleasure. Every Monday morning he goes to his publisher's office and picks up a pile of manuscripts that he will read and evaluate. He does this work for several hours in the morning. Afternoons, he goes for a walk, as is the case today. He visits antique dealers and auction houses so as to furnish the apartment he has just bought in Boulogne. While waiting to move there, he lives in two rooms lent by a friend, surrounded by boxes. Boulogne is not part of my territory, I cannot walk there. He is, however, an editor which makes me inclined to forgive many things.

When I ask him the name of the publishing house for which he works, he prefers not to answer. He has orders not to reveal the name of his employer. For him, it is an ethical question. I am a bit disappointed but his personality is not unpleasant. He is young. Perhaps too young? He is in a good mood because this morning at one of the shops of the Louvre des Antiquaires shops, he bought a small table in the Directory style which will go very well in his apartment with the Louis XVI wall sconces.

I brought with me the scrap book compiled about my two novels, containing all the reviews that I had. Fabien reads them with great interest. Those concerning my first novel are favorable and numerous. He studies them and has something to say about the journalists whom he knows. For a first effort, the novel was not bad. However, shortly thereafter, he comes to the only review concerning the second novel. It is a very short piece in *Le Monde.* It is very laudatory but it came out three months after the book was published. This fact does not escape his attention. He asks me why the review was so late in appearing and where are the other reviews?

- "The book came out in 1993, right in the middle of the election campaign for the House and Senate," I say. "There was no room in the newspapers for book reviews."

Fabien is not happy with this explanation.

- "Your editor has enough sense to avoid publishing during such a time. What happened?"

Now we are at the heart of the problem. This is what I had both hoped and feared. I ask myself if I would dare tell the real story explaining why my second novel had only one review. This explains why there has not been a third. I have never told the story to anyone. I am ashamed of what I did. But now, for the first time, I have a book editor in front of me. He seems to know the business and people in the business. He will be able to give me some advice.

- "It is all my fault," I begin by saying. "At the time I was quite difficult. I thought of myself as a great writer. My first novel, as you have seen, was a real critical success. But it took almost ten years to sell out the first printing. Despite that, since I wrote a second one, I believed that I was a success. I thought I was above criticism. They gave me a new press spokesperson. She had not read my book, which for me was an error. I was contemptuous towards her. It seemed to me that her work should be easy; the book reviewers knew me. She tried to explain to me that in ten years reviewers had moved on or had forgotten me. She tried to make me understand that it is impossible for a reputation to endure without being renewed. I refused to listen. She complained to the President who then called me in. He threatened to not publish the book. I was contemptuous towards him also. To treat your publisher like this was a capital sin. I had another argument with my press spokesperson, which accomplished nothing. Consequently the book came out at the worst possible time. When I asked to change the date of publication, the President growled, 'I warned you.' At the time, I did not see the trap but when I later rethought of the situation, I realized that they had set a trap for me and I fell right into it. When the short review in *Le Monde* was published it was already too late. All the copies had already been returned by the bookstores."

- "And the next novel?"

-"The publisher sent it right back to me and told me in no uncertain terms to find another publisher. The others are wary. An author who leaves his publisher after two novels with slow sales is a poor bet. They sent me polite rejection letters. And my bad luck continues; I get many compliments but no offers to be published. Yet, every time someone reads my books they are very pleased with them. It is a shame..."

I was satisfied with having said my piece but Fabien was not convinced. Being a book editor, he was sympathetic towards his colleagues. During my explanation I observed him moving backwards in his chair, stiffening his body, and avoiding looking at me. His attitude revealed his discomfort.

This was confirmed by his not looking at a copy of my second novel that I had placed on the table. There will be no second date. He was looking for a woman to decorate his new apartment; perhaps in front of the small Directory table and under the Louis XVI wall sconces. I overwhelm him with my problems; he only sees complications in me. He pays for my tea and steps out of my life.

It does not matter. I am not looking for an editor; I am looking for a companion. Fabien was not really compatible. I need more than him. I am not sorry to see him leave. As my mother said, after she asked the price of a dress that she admired in the window, "all things considered, the dress is really not that pretty", so it was with the book editor. I saw everything about him as negative.

To clear my mind and mood I decide to walk home. The rain had stopped. I circle the square behind Notre Dame and enter the small streets behind the Hotel de Ville which lead me to the Rue des Archives. I follow the Rue du Temple up to the Place de la République. I then plunge into the construction work that has made a mess of the Boulevard Magenta. It will be, I fear, a long time before we will see "the beautiful Magenta Walk" that the municipal authorities have promised for next year.

The telephone voice of Judge Philippe Massier is a bit slow but imposing. I find it hard to imagine how he looks. By the time I was ready to question him, he had already hung up. He telephoned me Thursday evening at six. I found his message when I got home and I immediately called him back. He invited me to the movies that very evening, at the Odeon Cinema in his neighborhood.

- "But if you have other plans...."

- "No, not at all. It will be a pleasure."

- "In the Place de l'Odéon there is a statue of Danton...."

- "If you say so...."

- "His hand is pointing toward the Rue de l'Ecole de Médecine. We can meet there; under Danton's hand at... let's say at 7:45. You choose the film."

The meeting place is romantic and I am charmed. I change in a hurry and wear my favorite color, green. I am right on time. I locate the statue and at 7:45 I am under Danton's hand. I have not yet realized that I am under Philippe's hand also. On the base of the statue, the famous sentence is engraved: "To defeat our country's enemies we must be daring, and daring and evermore daring. " I read further and learn that Danton said this in a speech to the Legislative Assembly on September 2, 1792.The statue is placed where Danton's house formerly stood. Around the statue's base there is a circular small stone bench, polished by use. Small groups of people speak to each other close to me. I make believe I am studying my *Pariscope*. I have already identified two or three movies whose starting time is convenient. I wait and wait. He has some nerve to be late, especially since he lives close. Finally, a man slips into place next to me.

- "Here I am." That is all he says. He gives me a chance to look at him.

He is not good looking. He is completely bald and he has three hairs on his nose. He looks like an ill-kept grade school teacher. He is dressed bizarrely; sneakers, wrinkled trousers, with a hole in the knee, and a rumpled seersucker jacket. He is sloppy but has a personal style. His voice is educated and his pronunciation clear and correct. We have to hurry. Together we choose a film and side by side we enter the MK2 movie theater. I have my monthly subscription pass so he will not have to pay for me. In a very short time we are seated in the dark and our glasses are in place. Immediately, we are in the middle of a Brian de Palma erotic scene featuring two women in the bathroom of a restaurant. Philippe leans back in his plush seat and stretches out his legs. He is rather uncomfortable which I find somewhat amusing. As I thought, he is a naughty boy, an adolescent spirit caught in an aging man's body. An hour and a half later we walk out and heave a sigh of relief.

- "Are we going to eat?" I ask with a certain false innocence.

- "I think we have to do so."

He is laughing. He is teasing me. I am very pleased. We wonder towards Boulevard Saint Michel and come to a Chinese restaurant where Philippe often eats. I would like to ask him a few questions but just as he did during our telephone conversation, Philippe takes over. He speaks about the Business Court and the cases he has to judge: the underhanded dealings, the tortured arguments there are made, and the problems of interpreting legal texts and precedents. Now that I am sitting across from him I note how heavy featured he is. When he stops talking he becomes ugly, but an interesting kind of ugly. As for the hairs on his nose...that can be remedied if he is willing.

While continuing his monologue, he eats his soup with rapidity. He talks on about lawyers, referred to as thieves, the huge sums of money that are disputed, his scummy colleagues, not all but some. He seems to criticize everyone. He is a big mouth. When he stops talking, his mouth turns downward, like a frown in a Greek theater mask. As we are leaving he insists on paying.

- "I much prefer to give up my money rather than my sperm," he says bizarrely to my confusion.

As we are walking, I continue to listen to him --he never seems to stop talking-- I watch how he walks. Our two shadows are poorly coordinated. However, later, I hold his hand so as to show others that though we are ill – assorted, we are together. I forget his sneakers and his too casual clothes. If he wants a second date, I will invite him to lunch. He says nothing. He accompanies me to the Saint Michel Metro Station and says he will call me. These are terrifying words; words that compel you to wait, to startle at each ring of the phone, and to continue to wait. I accept the situation. We give each other a friendly peck on the cheek and nothing more. Perhaps we will see each other again; perhaps not. I go down the steps to the Metro. This one I cannot rush. I have no others in sight. He is the last of the candidates. I remember that Friday he starts working and continues the weekend so as to prepare for Tuesday's cases. Undoubtedly, I will not hear from him before Monday evening. Already this seems to me to be a long time away. I look at my red date book -- too many empty pages. I have to make an effort to fill them.

Saturday I will go to the movies. Sunday morning I will distribute leaflets at the market. The afternoon, I do not know what to do. The only consolation is to write. And I must not forget to read.

When Monday arrives, I lose my patience. I refuse to wait any more. I call Philippe and ask him if I can come see him at work tomorrow at the Business Court. The sessions are open to the public. I will be discreet. He is curious. He says yes with a smile in his voice.

Monday evening, my mother calls me. I mistakenly tell her about Philippe. She is quite amused by the story. She informs me that she is not at all impressed by a Judge of the Business Court. If on the other hand, he was a Judge in the Juvenile Court or in the Criminal Court, she would… I answer by saying that next time I will take on a Judge from the former. She laughs. I do not find it so funny. In this search I have embarked on, I have invested all my energy and placed all my hopes. The quest, for the first time, has taken an unexpected hold on my life. This frightens me and yet gives me a reason to continue.

The following day at 11: 30 I show up at the Business Court on the Quai de la Corse. The huge court rooms, the giant stone staircase, the carved decorations from 1900, put me off a bit. I think of taking a small staircase which goes to the mezzanine. There is no one to ask for directions. I take the staircase and find a dead end. Downstairs again, I ask where Judge Massier is sitting? He is on the first floor but accessible only by the main staircase.

- "No matter what is discussed, you will understand nothing. It is a secret language," said Philippe on the telephone.

He then took the time to explain to me some of the main words used so that I could follow the arguments. The Court room is immense and tall. It is highly decorated. On the rear wall there are two oak banks of seats with backs. Each place is lit by a small lamp. In the crowd there are many women; as many in lawyer's robes as in street clothes. The lawyers parade about in black robes with white collars. At noon a bailiff announces: "The Court is now in session. All rise." He steps aside and five people enter the Courtroom. They also are dressed in shiny black robes with white trim. Their movements are measured and solemn. As they sit down, they slowly adjust their sleeves. The middle one with the shiny head is Judge Massier. I do not know if he sees me. He smiles to the public. He is very relaxed, just as he was in the restaurant. He seems to be at home. He has a few words for his colleagues to his left and to his right. The latter is a fat judge whose robe threatens to split under the pressure of his torso. The one on his left seems more friendly. The two others have their heads buried in their files.

- "The case Mornand-Lambert vs. Lepierre-Legendre is called," says a clerk from his oak box.

One lawyer comes in from the right. Another comes in from the left. Successively, each delivers a rapid fire argument of which, as predicted, I don't understand a word. I look at Philippe. His head is cocked to the side so as to hear better. He answers the lawyers with a few words. Undoubtedly, it is a case of false bankruptcies, theft, and misappropriations. Although it seems like a play, it is real. The parties do not really speak to each other. Each plays a set role. There is no human exchange. The money involved seems abstract. The legal terms and some of the names are impossible to pronounce. The brief exchange is over.

- "So be it..." says the Judge.

He never stops smiling. He is certainly an atypical judge. He knows the facts of the cases before him; he seems to be having a good time. The case is succeeded by another and then another. In an hour there are almost forty heard.

- "The case of Pochon-Meffrroi vs. Retier-Ledoux," says the clerk mechanically.

At the end of each presentation the Judge says,

- "Judgment will be rendered in two weeks".

Or else:

- "The case is carried over for one month."

Sometimes, Judge Massier hurriedly consults his colleagues I quickly understand why Philippe is so busy. These forty cases, each dealt with in a few minutes, determine the fate of wealthy shopkeepers and their less-well-off brethren. Once the judgment is rendered, no one dreams of arguing. As soon as they have finished talking the lawyers disappear as if magically erased. The man behind the oak pulpit has extraordinary power. All that can be seen are his head and his large mouth.

I am happy to have come. It is an exciting experience. This man, all the while smiling, who bends his head to listen, touches me. Even though in this setting he speaks little, he listens well and announces his decisions in a kind voice. It is not his job; he is not paid to do this; he is a volunteer. It was the first thing he told me when we first talked. He said it was traditional. All the judges in the Business Court are volunteers. They work on their assigned cases for days and sometimes weeks without compensation, for the prestige conferred by the position. For the power also I imagine. In an hour the Court adjourns; the five robed judges rise and leave; The spectators file out. I think Philippe during a moment recognized my presence in the courtroom. I was wearing green as I was at the Place de l'Odéon. I was sitting halfway back, alone on the long bench. I pause a bit before leaving. He catches up with me on the stairway. He has shed his robe and he looks at me with a smile.

- "So, Madame, what do you think about all this?"

Suddenly, he seems very young and in a very good mood. He did say that Tuesday evening, "I laugh, I run about, I dance." But it is not yet the evening and he is solicited by lawyers concerned with other cases. I give him a kiss on the cheek to say goodbye and I leave smiling. I want to know better the man I have just left. It seems now that all the effort and frustration, all the dates and dead ends, are to bear fruit.

I walk towards Notre Dame. I cross the Seine. I enter the cathedral; the shadows are dotted by candles. I make a tour of the aisles with a measured step. I like churches when they are empty; like the poetess Marceline Desbordes-Valmore. Notre Dame is certainly never empty. Groups of people whisper everywhere.

- "Let him be mine, I bespeak you."

I walk home via the Boulevard de Sébastopol and the Boulevard de Strasbourg.

Unfortunately, God does not see fit to control what happens in the bedroom. After the day at the Business Court there will follow several chaotic weeks during which Philippe and I are rarely in harmony. In bed and outside our relations are difficult. Our aging bodies have a problem in adjusting to the other.

There was the evening when he calls me an infantile leftist because I seek to explain why some youngsters become delinquents. I show him the door and throw his toothbrush in the garbage.

There was the morning when he comes in by train to the Gare de l'Est and surprises me with a visit to say hello. I buy another toothbrush.

There was the evening when I am tired of his comments about illegal immigrants and I reshow him the door and throw away a second toothbrush.

Then there was the morning when he phoned me and invited me to the Max Beckman exhibit at the Pompidou Center. I run out and buy a third toothbrush.

During all this, our physical relationship becomes worse and worse. Philippe's penis hardly moves in my hand. I no longer am able to awake him. One morning, while drinking his coffee, he solemnly covers my hand with his and proposes to me that we be only friends. Having no other choice, I accept. I have seen him little lately, I will in the future see him less. I do not know if he has already entered into that great sexual sleep that is old age, or if he wishes to be free of me. I will miss his vehemence.

Despite this experience, I soon thereafter mentally compose a new ad that I intend to place as quickly as possible. This time I chose *Fusac,* the magazine favored by foreigners living in Paris. It was how I made contact with Jean de Beaumont. Their personal column is very popular. It is a review filled with advertisements that serves to bring people together. Once again I say my prayers. I would really like to meet an American--.preferably a Jewish-American. I love their literature; it is full of life, tradition and feeling. There is also much attention to sex. I love their unique sensibility; their humor and self-mockery. In a word, I appreciate their humanity.

It is true that I desire to explore other possibilities and step away from my French contemporaries. I do not understand at all their sexual problems. I read somewhere that once Viagra came on the market it provoked a real revolution, even for men under fifty. I would like to find this reference and others. I type on the Internet, «The sexuality of older people. "I get 482,000 hits. It is an astounding mixture of advice on how to remain young and of things to buy so as to cure impotency. I narrow my search to the year 2007. 246,000 hits. I look at the first ones which are supposed to be the most pertinent. I find a study on the sexual behavior of the French, from which it is impossible to extract information about the over sixty. There is a training course offered on the care of the geriatric population; a study on institutionalized old people; different publications on aging and old age; an invitation to a seminar at Villefranche sur Saône... After two hours of navigating I have not found a serious study on the subject that interests me.

I go to the research library at the Pompidou Center. I question a young man sitting at the social science information desk. He responds by typing something on his computer keyboard and then tells me in a regretful tone:

- "I am so sorry Madame, we have nothing on the

subject."

- "What? There were 482,000 hits on the Internet and you have nothing!"

Between clenched teeth he mutters the words "Internet" and "garbage" and re-attacks his computer. Several manipulations later he hands me a sheet of paper with the following references:

-Danon-Boileau, Henri. *De la vieillesse à la mort,* (From Old Age to Death). Calmann-Levy, 2000.

What a wonderful beginning! Fortunately the following books are a bit more upbeat.

-Friedan, Betty. *La révolte du Troisième Age,* (The Fountain of Age) Albin Michel, 1995.

- Henrard, Jean-Claude. *Les défis du vieillissement,* (The Challenges of Aging) La Découverte 2002.

- Collange, Christiane. *La deuxième vie des femmes,* (The Second Life of Women) Laffont/Fayard, 2005.

- Sansot, Pierre. *Les vieux, ça ne devrait jamais vieillir,* (Old People Should Never Get Old). Payot 1995.

For several of the following afternoons I go to the Pompidou Center to study these works as well as others in the same section. I learn a lot about aging and useful things to adopt so as to stay young; but I find almost nothing about the love life of the elderly. In the book by Danon-Boileau I find the reference to the Viagra revolution. It is an expensive revolution because this drug is not covered by the National Health Service. Fortunately, it will soon be generically available.

Betty Friedan's book is a 500 pages hymn singing the praises of old age and old people. Its purpose is to prove that there is no decline in the creativity of people during the last years of their life. She shows that, but has very little interest in what she calls the "intimate parts" of life. She lost her husband when she was in her sixties and did not feel the need to fill that part of her life. It is true, as some nasty people say, that she was extraordinarily ugly.

As for Christiane Collange, her habitual optimism prevents her from looking at the bed of the women that she studies. Those whom she actually spoke with have little opportunity, she says, to find a new partner after their divorce or widowhood and do not seem to wish for another. In the other works, the subject is not tackled.

Another book, *Vivre en maison de retraite,* (Life in a Retirement Home), Presses Universitaires de France, 2002, looks at the reality of residents in "their final home", an institution. Around half a million people live in such places in France. There is not one word on their sexual behavior. However, we know that their desires are far from being nonexistent and that living with people of the opposite sex can only stimulate such desires. Scenes of individuals masturbating have been reported in some television documentaries. The contributors to the book ignore or suppress the subject of sexual activities.

A love life is of concern to 55% of the women and 75% of the men over 70 according to an American study cited by *Santé* in a channel 5 program in 2006. Where are these people? What taboo prevents them from showing themselves or speaking out? Why this silence about an activity sometimes considered as the essential quality of humankind? Why, once someone is older than 60, do they no longer have the right to discuss something that makes life enjoyable and pleasurable? The sexual life of men and women can continue up to the very end of their life. Pleasure does not cause wrinkles so long as we take our time and trust in ourselves. And what if love is the privilege of old age?

As I do every year on July 2, I dress in black and go to the Place de la Concorde in answer to the call of all the groups which fight for the total elimination of the Death Penalty. I am part of a "die in" as is called this demonstration on the date when the moratorium on the sentence was lifted in the USA. This end of the moratorium took place on July 2, 1976 and the first execution following this was that of Gary Gilmore on January 17, 1977 in the state of Utah. We gather at 6 P.M on the Rue Saint Florentin, a few yards distant from the annex of the American Embassy.

When I get there, I get on line in front of a table on which white masks and black armbands. Are piled up. On the latter, in large letters is a name and the death date of someone executed since the end of the moratorium. We put on the mask and slip on the armbands. There is total silence. We are more than a hundred all wearing black pants and T-shirts. A voice over the loud speaker reviews the major events in the history of the Death Penalty in America, followed by the calling of the role of those names written on our armbands. When the name on your arm is announced, each demonstrator lays down and remains motionless. The names go on; seemingly endlessly. Bit by bit the ground is covered with black clad white masked bodies. When everyone is accounted for, the silence is quiet moving. We all think about the meaning of this ceremony and the fate of the executed. I concentrate on all those American men and women, mostly Black, who have fallen during these years.

Then the demonstrators get up and the action is over.

Every year I note that the ground is further away, the pavement harder, and my arms and legs less flexible. It is now time to return my props and find my friends. Amnesty International, The League of Human Rights, Together against the Death Penalty, ACAT, The Catholic Association Against Torture and the Struggle For Justice are all present. We are glad to be able to rid ourselves of our emotional overload; we discuss and exchange flyers. It is an opportunity to make new contacts. My friend Aline Montfort, from the Struggle For Justice, introduces me to a young American. He runs a theater group which puts on plays opposing the death penalty. We make an appointment to meet later. I say hello to my friends in Amnesty International. This demonstration is the only one which manages to bring together very different groups often at odds with one another even though they have a common aim. An hour later I go home under a still bright July sky. I was dead for a few minutes in the Place de la Concorde; I am now happy to be alive. Lights begin to brighten the display windows of the Place Vendôme.

The pick-up is a complex operation. You have to be daring and ever more daring, as Danton said; in addition, you need stamina and tenacity. Above all, you must have much self-confidence. It seems to me that women are far from equal to men in this area. Following the advice of my friend Isabelle, I made several attempts to attract the attention of the opposite sex.

- "You walk around museums and you hang around cafés," Isabelle advised me.

I understand that. But how do I avoid being arrested for solicitation? How can I be smiling and inviting in public without running the risk of being taken for a prostitute? Twice, I had the opportunity to pick up a man. I seized the chance. All I received for my efforts was a humiliation.

At the Fornay Library one afternoon I found seated across from me, just a bit to my right, a good looking man with the face of an intellectual, long gray hair and a well chiseled nose. I stared at him while he worked on a manuscript. Suddenly he glanced up and irritably looked at me. It was as if another women had just tried the same maneuver. I refused to meet his glance. I fled by, looking at the book open before me.

My second effort took place during a political meeting. A tall handsome man with an aristocratic head was sitting behind a table a few yards away from me. I glanced at him several times. At first he avoided my look. Encouraged, I took the chance to continue glancing at him. He turned towards me and lifted his chin so suddenly that it seemed to me as if he had struck me. I lowered my head; I blushed and was incapable of looking up during the rest of the meeting. While leaving, as bad luck would have it, we came face to face. I still could not make myself look any higher than his chest. He had a motorcycle helmet in his hand. I was so confused that I could only look up after he had left.

Sometimes I try to pick someone up during a demonstration or a march, but I have not often met men of my age in these circumstances. The supposedly stronger sex is sloppily dressed. They are not very sexy. Banners and signs do not lend themselves to light-hearted banter. Moreover, far from showing themselves flattered by the unprovoked attention, men often display irritation and sometimes anger because I look at them. It seems that their masculine ego reacts poorly to my initiatives and undoubtedly they are afraid of being treated as sex objects.

Still, from time to time, I smile at men in the Metro to thank them, as they are younger than me, for giving me their seats.

I have not spoken of my tears, tears of sadness and pain that I shed each time that I lose a man. I do not give in to them often; tears make for wrinkles and fever blisters. They make you ugly. They scar the eyelids and cause crow's-feet. For twenty years after my tenth birthday I cried very seldomly. I renewed my acquaintance with tears in my thirties.

The first man who took me in his arms was my boss. I was his secretary. An encounter that was crucial in determining my life. He taught me a profession that enabled me later to work in interesting jobs, but he was also the man who destroyed me sexually. He was the man who for a long time caused me to be frigid; who thus thrust me into a fruitless search for sexual pleasure. This is a condition that psychiatrists call by the nasty name of erotomania. My children can never understand my life if they do not give proper place to this search of mine which was the motor driving my life and the cause of my instability.

His name was Monsieur Serpentin. He was 52 and I was 18. I was looking for a job as a stenographer -typist in a textile company near the Champs Elysées. The Personnel Director called me for an interview. He was a busy little man who gave me a typing test. Computers of course were in the future and corrections were not permitted. I was not perfect but I was hired because of my persona. I had spent a year learning stenography in a school near the Opera. I was not good for very much but I was eager to learn. I had my

Baccalaureate Degree and had been thoroughly enchanted by my major in Philosophy. Despite this, I was happy to be looking for work. I realized that the death of my father forced me to earn my own living and I was not mad at my mother for being unable to continue my studies. It was the exciting sixties and the world of work was enticing.

I had been working for a half an hour when Monsieur Serpentin showed up. His quick heavy steps in the hallway announced his arrival. When he entered the room my first thought was, "he is the boss. I would not like to get on his bad side..." He was heavily built; almost obese. He had a gray mustache yellowed by tobacco and a cheeked suit that threatened to burst at the seams in an instant. He shook my hand and welcomed me to the company. I was surprised to find his hand cool and firm. He said hello to the other workers and had something personal to say to each one. I said to myself that it would be perhaps not unpleasant to work with him. He then went into his office. Every morning he showed up at 9:30 and I did not see him again for the rest of the day. His secretary, Michelle, worked next to me. In the morning she went into his office for an hour and returned with a steno-book filled with jottings that she alone could read. I worked for newly hired members of the sales force. Hardy France Inc. was a branch of an English concern that produced artificial and synthetic fibers. Our company had been formed to market in France Fibrelle, an acrylic fiber whose properties were similar to those of the French Crylor and the German Goslan. The letters I typed were now well done. I learned how to file and answer the telephone. Several months later Michelle became pregnant and I replaced her. Now it was my turn to go into Monsieur Serpentin's office every morning to take his correspondence. It was a promotion that made me happy. Little by little during our morning sessions my boss took the time to speak to me about the recipients of his letters and the situations surrounding them. He profiled portraits of his business relations and confided in me his professional hopes. Later on, he spoke of the technical aspects of his business. I eagerly listened to him. He spoke of the great textile dynasties as if they were part of his family and as if he, a man from the North of France, had always lived among them. He sketched for me charts illustrating relations between different competitors. He liked to draw so as to complement his explanations, retouching the outline of a loom or sketching a diagram of a spinning machine. My stays in his office went on and on; soon I spent the whole morning there. Gradually my confidence increased and I made up simple letters to clients. I undertook to change the file system. Co-workers sometimes made suggestive remarks about our time together. But with my lipstick untouched and my virtue intact they hesitated to go further in their insinuations.

One day Monsieur Serpentin invited me to lunch. We ate oysters and drank too much Muscadet. Going back to the office he grabbed my hand and kept hold of it. I said to myself that it was only a hand that it was not serious, and I let him keep hold of it. Consequently every morning he appropriated my fingers during all the time spent dictating letters. Our lunches were more frequent. Coming back from the restaurant in the car he tried to kiss me. I had more and more trouble defending myself. I knew he was married to a woman from the North and had four children. It was out of the question for me to have an affair. It was absurd to think of him getting a divorce; he was much too old for me. Yet, little by little, he gained ground. First the lips were conquered, then the breasts. Surrender was near. During all this he continued to teach me. Soon I was able to stop being a secretary and was put in charge of sales promotion for Fibrelle's woman's clothing department. I had my own office and personal business cards. Despite being the chosen prey of Monsieur Serpentin, I tried to resist. One day, he reserved a room in the Auberge de la Poularde in the Chevreuse Valley. After an elaborate meal he laid me down on the bed and proceeded to devour me. All I felt was disgust and it became worse when he got on top of me and cried:

- "I am in your hole! Finally I am in your hole!"

Months went by without me having the least bit of sexual pleasure. I became more and more frigid. However, I knew that I was not completely without feeling. There had been a little spark several days after he had taken me; but rather than becoming a small fire, the spark was extinguished.

We continued to work together. Monsieur Serpentin now took me with him to visit spinning and weaving factories. Then he let me go off on my own. I made a trip to visit clothing factories on the Côte d'Azur. I drove along the Corniche in a red Renault Floride convertible that I had rented. I was almost happy despite the voice of Monsieur Serpentin in the evening over the telephone. I knew that when I returned I would have to fall again under his control. I had slipped into a sick relationship and I no longer dared to look at what had become my life. My first husband, Eric, a year later, came and pulled me out of my swamp.

The evening of our first meeting, Eric Descoins implored me to break immediately with Monsieur Serpentin. He presented me with the telephone and made very obvious his intention to listen to my conversation. I obeyed him. I knew he was right. A bit shakily I called my former boss to tell him that we would not be seeing each other again. Undoubtedly because his wife was there he could not argue. The operation was less than courageous but it worked and the conversation was brief. Eric and I laid down still clothed and I sensed the little spark return.

Fibrelle did not have the anticipated success on the French market; consequently the parent company reduced the work force of its branch. Monsieur Serpentin and I were among the first laid off. My textile background allowed me to join, almost immediately, the Public Relations Department of the advertising giant Publicis. The result was less happy for my boss. He was unemployed at fifty plus and it pained me to see him like this. He had been very hurt by his dismissal and I had believed that it was not the right time to leave him. I had been even more caught up in his affaire because Monsieur Serpentin had brought me into his family. I went on vacation with his children; I chatted with his wife; I played bridge with his friends. The situation was both exciting and impossible. My meeting Eric, who was at the time a young Publicity Director, was the solution that I had hoped for. I admired that he was strong enough to pry me loose from the trap I was in.

He made me laugh with his imitations of Laurel and

Hardy. He was never short of funny comments. It was a talent he inherited from his singer and actor father, who was also an exceptional imitator. Eric, at eighteen, attempted to become a theatrical professional. The death of his father brought to an abrupt halt this ambition. He was forced to support himself and his mother, Blanche, who lived with him. During our honeymoon we began to look for a house in the Loire Valley and subsequently we spent all our week-ends searching in the countryside around Blois.

Our sex life, however, after our marriage, was a disaster. The first time I slept with Eric his bossy ways repelled me. Lying on top of me, this time naked, he said to me:

- "Don't move, don't do anything, you don't know anything."

These words froze me. I was forbidden to budge. They chased away any hope of desire. Once again I felt nothing while making love and I silently screamed out my anger. We had bought a house at Mont-près-Chambord; our marriage was scheduled for the coming months. I thought our sexual relations would improve with time.

Three years later we decided to leave Paris and move permanently to our country house. Eric quit his job and began to prepare for our new life. We had a son and I made the weekend commute by car with him. Saturday and Sunday we showed Parisian potential buyers farms and country houses. Our business grew and I left Publicis. We worked full time and lived well thanks to our real estate business.

Despite this, our sex life grew worse and worse. We made love rarely and without pleasure. Eric spent more and more time in the bathroom and I likewise masturbated. He began to chase my friends from Publicis who came to spend a weekend. Saturday evenings he took them to the Château de

Chambord to "show them the deer." They came back not saying anything and unable to look at me. "The deer thing" became a workplace joke between us. The political and social earthquake of May 1968 had seismic consequences. Little by little the idea of leaving Eric and going back to Paris took hold. A friend offered to let me stay in her house in a western suburb. I left with my four year old son. As I put him in the car and loaded our luggage, I was overcome with a feeling of desperation and defeat. For the first time in years I cried and I continued to cry up to our arrival. I thought that something in me was missing and would never be found. I was thirty years old, however, and hope was still possible.

When I left Eric I had made him promise to see a psychiatrist; I told him I would perhaps return if he changed his behavior. I felt strongly that I also needed a psychiatrist. When Jean-Pierre called me to schedule an appointment to speak with me about my husband, I immediately fell in love with him.

Jean-Pierre's lab coat was open on his brown corduroy suit. He had a tan shirt and a brown tie decorated with little tan and white fox heads. The first thing that attracted me to him was the refinement of his clothing. Our appointment lasted more than an hour. He questioned me about my husband's behavior and his personality. He was kind and discreet. He did not touch on difficult subjects and avoided speaking of our sex life. I felt grateful to him for his tact. He lit his pipe, looked at me with compassion, made his notes with an elegant hand, and excused himself when he interrupted me. We were supposed to have another appointment a month later and I waited impatiently for this second encounter. When it finally arrived, I dressed with care. Once again, I went to the big hospital in Garches. Again, I went down corridors and crossed trolleys occupied by prone but smiling patients. I spent an hour and a half in the waiting room. I was ready to leave when finally the Doctor showed up and excused himself with this sentence I will never forget.

- "I have the same sort of problems as you."

These few words freed my hopes and permitted me to dream. Our session was shorter than the first but he promised me there would be a third.

Unable to wait, several days later, I daringly took the initiative. I sent him a letter in the format of a questionnaire and asked him to strike out the inappropriate responses. It was a way to invite him to dinner. That weekend I went to Mont-près-Chambord with my son Lucien. I slipped and fell, and badly scraped my right hand. Upon my return I found the completed questionnaire of Jean-Pierre under the salutation:

- "My dear Nutty Lady."

He invited me to spend the following weekend in Amsterdam, Holland. I left my son with his father and we spent our first night at an apartment lent to Jean-Pierre by some friends in the Saint Germain-des-Prés neighborhood. The windows faced the Boulevard Saint Germain. He jokingly asked me how I managed to scrape the hand that had written the letter of invitation. He was a psychiatrist even during his non-working hours.

The next morning we set out for Holland. We arrived there and found a fog so dense that we were forced to look for our hotel for several hours in this eerie atmosphere. I swam in a vast formless ocean of happiness. Sunday, the sun came back and we visited the Rijksmuseum where, before the Rembrandt painting called "The Jewish Fiancée," which features a rich happy couple, I broke down in tears. I had finally found my way and the little spark so often extinguished had become a great fire of joy.

We had a dozen delicious years together. Our sexual relations were excellent even though I never had an orgasm. That seemed to me of little importance. We raised a family consisting of my son, the two daughters of Jean-Pierre and his first wife, his son, by his mistress, who I loved very much, and a son of our own. Jean-Pierre had advised me to leave Lucien with his father during the week. Together Jean-Pierre and I added a fifth child, Adam, who was for me a marvel. The two girls were pretty and affectionate and the Christmas and Easter holidays a joy. We were very happy up to the moment that my erotomania intervened and put an end to this endless honeymoon.

The Devil's Servant appeared in the body of a very handsome politician who would later become a Government Minister. His name was Robert Aubiet and when I met him he was a leader of a political faction of growing importance. He stood for a third position between Left and Right. I had participated in a three day retreat in the Luberon Mountains and it was love at first sight. Robert made advances which were sexually loaded. During a meeting of movement members he stood before me and invited me to admire him from top to bottom; especially the bottom. The great fire, which had been banked by the years, flamed up again. I was forty two years old and had still never had an orgasm with a man. I saw in him my last chance. I had to seize it.

All these sexual overtures led nowhere. Robert did not like women. I had been told that but I did not believe it. How could someone be so cruel? Later on I learned that Robert made a habit of sexually encouraging all the women in his entourage. Strangely, a few became his mistresses. He even ended up married when he became Minister, undoubtedly to give a normal appearance to his life. He destroyed mine and he still today does not realize it.

I took my son Adam with me and moved to an apartment a few miles from the City Hall where Robert was Mayor as well as National Representative. I ran into him from time to time in meetings. He came towards me and shook my hand with that look that people show to very sick people who are unaware of how desperate is their situation. I was incapable of realizing that he had used me for his political benefit and made me into one of his many groupies. I still expected a miracle. I went looking for the man who Robert was in love with. As luck would have it, I found him by chance. We had a conversation which lasted all night and after, I went directly to the hospital. They treated my depression with a sleep cure. Upon my discharge, several weeks later, my son Adam saved me by asking me if we could go back and live with his father. This we did. In the six months since my leaving, I had began to draw up and paint. An exhibit at the Cergy Pontoise Library marked the end of my stay.

Jean-Pierre had waited for me but he had also taken a mistress. She was non-demanding for two years and then she decided to get rid of me. She thought up all sorts of ways: She sent me nude photos of herself taken in our bedroom with Adam's picture visible above her head. Because the doors of our house were never locked, she could come as she pleased and did so several times; she took baths or turned off the heat. She telephoned me several times a day and hung up as soon as she heard my voice. Jean-Pierre did nothing to stop her. I made two attempts at suicide. It was during this time that I had the disagreements with my publisher. It became unbearable. This situation continued for several years. With age, Adam found the atmosphere at home more and more impossible. . As soon as he was eighteen he left. Jean-Pierre decided to do likewise.

My ad in *Fusac* which came out three days ago was a surprise to me. It came out in the Friendship section. It listed an E-Mail address. I received three replies on my computer. The first came from Maryk, a 32 years old Syrian in Paris for his dental studies. The second was from a Libyan law student who promised me a trip to his country. The third was the most noteworthy. It was a declaration of love. He is 28 years old, a Tunisian who does not tell me what he does for a living but swears to me that he will take me on "a love adventure that will lead me to paradise." This, despite the fact that my age, 69, is prominent at the beginning of my ad. I am bewildered. Once again, it is my friend Isabelle who clears up the confusion.

- "Take it easy. It's obvious; they want to marry you so as to get resident status.

That's all..."

Curiosity might have made me answer these three young men. I was right in resisting the temptation.

I receive the letter in the middle of July. It was forwarded to me by *Fusac*. It is written in French.

First of all, I congratulate you on your courage in admitting that you are 69. I am sending you the enclosed photograph in the hope that you will agree that I am younger than my 65 years.

I also like art exhibits, classical music as well as everything connected with food and wine, walking, running, and reading.

An American by birth, I am a Parisian by adoption. I am a widower without children. I am looking with much hesitation and some timidity to find again an emotional life. I admit to being lost and out of touch with the man-woman game. As a result I ask in advance for your pardon should I commit serious errors. As for the other conditions that you requested: Yes, I am slim (155 lbs. For 5'9"). Alas, I am single –too single. Cultivated? Not as much as I would like. I was a University Professor. I have a doctorate and have written. Movies? Not at all. But don't you think life is made for learning?

If this profile is of interest to you, please call me and we can further discuss the questions involved. Hope to hear from you soon,

William

The warm and sincere tone of this letter pleases me immediately. I like also the little notes of confusion. Above all, I am attracted by the willingness to learn and the openness of the communication.

That very evening I call William and meet his American accent. I immediately fall in love with this accent during the long conversation which follows where we touch all the bases.

Two years ago, he lost his wife to lung cancer. He is a New Yorker, born in the Bronx. He taught History at the City College of the City University of New York. His full name is William Cohen. A New York Jew. It is too good to be believed. I had dreamed about such a person. I do not tell him that. Unfortunately, he has to leave for a week's visit in the Nantes area. We make a date for right after his return: July 27 at 10 A.M. in front of the Guimet Museum. They are exhibiting a series of Japanese etchings. For me the subject is very suggestive. Did he get the salacious reference? Later on he will tell me he did. For the immediate, we are both charmed. He lives in the 8th Arrondissement, not too far from the Museum.

A whole week to wait. His photo is attractive. He is really quite slim and looks in good shape. He is wearing a pale pink shirt and cut off jean shorts. He looks like a teenager with his rain jacket around his waist. Sun glasses hide his eyes. His brown hair is cut very short. Over the telephone, when asked what was his hair color he said, "dirty blonde." He is not afraid to mock himself. I like that. Capping it all off is his big smile; a huge very American smile, just like Humphrey Bogart.

When I find him in front of the Guimet Museum, he is leaning against an iron fence and looking about with a lost look. As usual, I was early and I was waiting for him in the short line at the top of the steps. He shows up early also and is surprised that I am likewise. As soon as I introduce myself he rediscovers his smile. It is a smile that is open, all-encompassing and contagious. It puts me immediately in a good mood. I recognize him by his clothing; the same pink shirt and jean. We go into the museum and stop for a coffee. Once seated, we take the time to look at each other. The photo is a good, recent likeness. I am not disappointed. I tell him that he has a very American look. He answers by telling me that for the most part Americans are more solidly built than him. He speaks French very well. I am not going to improve m my English much. We laugh together. Then it is time to go see the exhibit.

In the first room I literally fall into his arms. While looking at the etchings we bump into one another and end up intertwined. He is pleased. Several times he will collide with me. Later he will tell me that he felt a gravitational pull working on him. We study these Japanese prints together. They are mannered and almost always the same during several centuries. There is the same female face with a small red mouth, the same eyes, the same scary Samouris. Hiroshige, Hokusaï, and Utamaro have continued a tradition and popularized the stereotypes. Unfortunately there are no erotic pictures; just landscapes. William closely studies the prints. He wants to see everything.

An hour and half later we leave the Museum with a light step and open to all possibilities. He suggests that we have a drink. I propose that we have it in his place since he lives close by. He is at ease with the idea. A good sign. Many men are uneasy with the prospect of showing their quarters because of "the mess." We take a bus which passes by the Parc Monceau. This time I want to put my head on his chest. We are on the same page all the time together. We get to his building and I find a luxurious marble lobby. It is a lovely apartment in the traditional style. There are lace curtains and many small wooden framed pictures. We visit the apartment. The paintings and sketches are almost all the work of his mother who went to Art School. The furniture is made from exotic wood. I will later learn that he built it himself. He proudly shows me the kitchen. It is his kingdom. There are shiny copper pots and pans of all sizes and shapes hanging on the walls. There is a stove fit for a restaurant; knife racks everywhere as well as all sorts of kitchen utensils. He opens the refrigerator and pulls out a half-bottle of Champagne. "There is always a chilled bottle," he says with a big smile. There are almost 70 years of life to talk about. I do not repeat myself. He looks at me with an ever changing regard. He talks to me about his wife, Joy, whom he cared for up to the last moment. For 45 years he never kissed another woman. She was his only love. William's face is the mirror of his emotions, he cannot lie; he goes from sadness to elation in a second. Certainly the Champagne helps create an atmosphere. However, the happiness of this meeting plays a big role. As time passes, we grow hungry. He invites me into the kitchen. He finds some tomatoes and slices them with precision. I discover that he is a Chef. He continues his demonstration of technique with an onion and a cucumber. He then goes to pick herbs from his window box. With a final flourish, he pulls out of the refrigerator a full cheese plate, each variety wrapped in paper. And there is bread; real bread.

We picnic in the dining room. The walls are decorated with objects connected to the vine and to wine tasting. There is a collection of corkscrews and other accessories unknown to me.

- "I love wine," William says in all simplicity.

His paternal grandfather was a wine grower and maker. There are photos of vineyards on the walls of the dining room. Coffee is served in porcelain cups. Nearly fifteen of these cups and saucers, all different, are hanging in a display cabinet. He is a man who loves his home and is caring and watchful of his nest.

I leave right after eating. I want to be at the Pompidou Library before it gets too crowded. We make a date for a lunch at my place. Go step by step I tell myself, do not rush things. My head is deliciously light because of the Champagne.

I have little memory of the lunch in my apartment. My head is elsewhere. I am so overwhelmed by worry about my cooking that I do not hear a word of what William tells me. He is a Chef; I must try to measure up to him. I prepare for him a salmon dish with fennel and ginger pears for desert. I know that he does not like chocolate. How can someone not love chocolate?

I hardly talk about my two marriages. He prefers to regard the pictures on the wall. They are the only oil paintings that I kept after my exhibit in the Val-d'Oise. I sold the sketches and almost all the pastels, at a ridiculously low price. The oils however I did not wish to give up. They took me too much time to do. Undoubtedly, I will never again do such work. William compliments everything as a guest should and announces with pleasure that I "have a nice home." With his accent the phrase is charming and almost funny. We walk along the Saint Martin Canal and continue on to the Place de la Bastille where we separate. We are both very pleased with our stroll. He walks well; that is encouraging. We made a date for another lunch. This time at his place, the Rue du Rocher.

The day of that lunch we do not finish our meal. After the first few bites, William gets up and looks at me with that distressed stare born of desire. I hardly have the time to ask him if he has a prophylactic. He leads me to the bedroom. The bed is covered with a white crocheted spread, the window is decorated with blue drapes. I undress in the semi-darkness. It is wonderful to fill in my arms a thin and supple body, like a climbing plant. And I am delighted to see him set off in search of my own. He kisses every part that his lips touch. He caresses, he licks, he sucks all of me. My American lover is very thorough. He was in a hurry to get to the bedroom. Once there, he takes his time, he becomes meticulous. He travels about me, he learns about me, he discovers me. Then it is my turn to find him, to excite him, to raise higher his passion. We are thirty years old, then we are twenty. And finally when he enters me I feel a lively and alert penis, an almost boyish member which takes me with conviction.

Love making with him is like a horse race. It is a headlong run at full speed by a thorough bred skillfully mounted. He flies over obstacles, he dashes by barriers, he fords rivers and comes at last to the finish line. He lets loose the reins and rests for a moment. But only for a moment. To my great surprise I feel him harden again and reawaken. For the first time in my life I witness a second bout of love making, followed by a third. My vigorous partner, that I believed sated, rises up from his slumber and attacks anew. His second engagement is more imperious than the first. One again he jumps over hedges, clears hurdles and arrives at the finish all sweaty. A few seconds of rest and it is time for the third campaign. This time he is quieter and more reserved. The ground is heavy, the hooves weighty but victory is none the less his. Finally, all used up, and scoured dry; he collapses in my arms, exhausted and happy. I dry the sweat along his back.

When I praise him for his performance, he says:

- "You should have seen me when I was young,"

I then explain to him that for me a man could only have a single ejaculation. My mother taught me nothing about this. Books never said a word about it. The men that I have known were content with a single orgasm. Modestly, he sighs and I will learn nothing more about his exploits.

The next morning, holding hands, we are on line at the Aids Detection Center at the Fernand Widal Hospital. It is a free and anonymous procedure. I have already made this journey twice before and the nurses make believe that they do not know me. It is a simple blood test and the results will be available next week. William is anxious. His recent contacts with hospitals were such that he is struck by very bad memories. He stays close to me and is upset when a nurse makes me go in alone into a treatment room. I cannot even reassure him with a gesture as the door is already closed. Fortunately, it is not long and it is soon his turn. He takes courage when he sees me calmly awaiting his return. The Doctor does not know me. I will not have to explain myself. I do not want to tell anyone that I have changed sex partners three times in a few months. I insist that sexual relations and the corollary VIH test are indispensable. I meet my William who is a bit shaken but happy that it is over. The results, as we were sure they would be, are negative. Armed with this knowledge we can be rid of prophylactics, those "erection stranglers" as my dear American calls them.

Everything has gone so fast, we hardly know one another and yet I sense that all is already in place. This time it is going to work; this is going to last. In the following days, a shared desire pulls us together. At the movies, in a museum, in a restaurant, we cannot get enough of each other. We hold hands, we constantly look at each other. I cannot stop staring at him. We laugh together all the time. Only our advances age keeps us from going further. We cannot forget that he is 65 years old and I am 70 - although I swear I am 69. 69 is the erotic number, I knew it would bring me luck and happiness. I intend to stay 69 as long as possible. We do not kiss in public. William has decided on this policy. To do so would be flaunting and provocative. We are restrained. The days follow one another and reveal to each of us more of the other. Sometimes it is at my place, other times it is in his apartment. Between the Rue des deux gares and the Rue du Rocher there are several Metro stations. I have still not tried to walk the distance, I am in too much of a hurry to get there. And then there is our first separation. I am going away on vacation with Lucien and Laura and my two grand-sons for three weeks.

We make the trip by car and stop in the Drome Department to see Jean-Pierre and his new wife, Sarah. They graciously welcome us. I have not burnt my bridges with them although we have lived together through difficult moments. They prepare for us a delicious Provençal meal, featuring a Gaspacho and a vegetable Tian. Sarah is completely different from me; she is a good looking black haired, extroverted woman who acts in a community theater with Jean-Pierre. We leave the following morning.

I write to William almost every day. We call each other on our cell phones. Because he cannot send letters to the address of my former in-laws, he keeps a daily journal. After three days I want to leave the beach and rush back to Paris by the first available train. And yet, these days are sweet because I see my children on vacation, relaxed and happy. We eat together. It is a pleasure to walk to the port of Saint Tropez at 8 AM and buy a newspaper, followed by a coffee at the Gorille Café--even though it is no longer called The Gorille - and then go back slowly before it gets crowded. I enjoy spending my afternoons under the pine trees, a book on my knees, watching the squirrels jump from branch to branch. In the evening I get together with Clement when he comes back from the beach and read to him one at a time all the chapters of his first real book *Un bon petit diable.* And at the end of the day, after dinner, I go back with my flash light to "my place "with the scent of the pines. I sleep in my handsome Provençal cottage, loaned to me by my mother in law, all alone in a young girl's bedroom decorated with golden angels. And like a smitten young girl I think of William as I fall asleep and mentally write the letter that I will send him the next morning. I choose the most optimistic and reassuring words. I rehearse the few words that I will leave as a message on his answering machine; the story that will make him laugh. With my thoughts full of my partner, his face filling my eyes, and the memory of his body in my hands, I fall asleep with desire and need inside me.

Extracts from William's "diary".

August 17

You are lucky. You have an address to write to. All I have is white sheet paper. Despite that, when I think of you, when I write to you (even if these words are not posted), I feel close to you. That makes me very happy. The first little week is over. I had the enormous pleasure to get two letters from you. You spoil me. The first week-end apart was less difficult than I feared. It is as if the thought that we have found each other was enough to calm me. I have not suffered the pain of loneliness, the waves of sadness, the shocks of loss, or the sense of desertion which have visited me these last years. Your presence, or rather your absence, certainly weighed on me. But your existence, the fact of you, the memory of our shared time together, counterbalanced the other. I thus achieved a sort of equilibrium which left me calm and composed. As a result, the week-end of the 15 August went well enough. I was alone for the time. I made several phone calls, a few people called me, yet for the three days I spoke to no one, except for two or three minutes with the cheese lady and likewise with François. Everyone was gone. I survived. An important step for me. I thank you. Look what you have done. Thanks.

August 19

A sad, sad day. A low dark gray sky. Rain. Despite this, I am not too bad. I miss you a lot. Still, I have some pep. I am not paralyzed by my depression. I talk to you often. I ask you a question; I share with you an observation. Did you notice that in the film *Les poupées russes,* there are at least two, perhaps three or four, scenes shot at the intersection of Boulevards Raspail and Montparnasse? That is to say, in front of the Bar à Huitres Restaurant (where we ate together on the eve of your departure). I liked your account of that Friday evening. I would have noted the breakfast together Saturday morning as well as your hand on my thigh during the car ride coming and going. These are memories to squirrel away. (I don't think this is a verb; it should be). I have only these things to warm me during the coming two weeks.

August 20

You spoil me. A postcard and a letter this morning! Just like children do with their gifts, I let them sit in the mail box until I came back from my run. The card was quickly digested in the elevator. The letter was sipped like an after-dinner drink after my shower. It was at that moment that I realized that I am happy. What a strange feeling! Not one I have experienced in a long time. Its a state where I find mixed together a portion of peace, a dash of calm, and a good dose of contentment. It is a dish I will savor in the coming days.

August 21

A cloudy day. When will we see summer? I lived through a Saturday evening alone. The second in a row; after so many months trying to avoid this. The Anna effect produces peace and a certain feeling of well-being. Being alone no longer frightens me; or at least does so much less. Which is not to say that I would not prefer to have you - in flesh and bone - beside me.

August 22

It is good; it is great that you like to walk. I invite you to get lost in Paris. Strolling hand in hand in places unknown to us, seldom visited and little noted —what a pleasure! It is the same with your answering machine. Hearing your voice consoles me but leaves me unsatisfied. Half the separation is behind us. It is hard; like I am when I think of you.

August 23

I cannot get the hang of my cell phone. You just called me. I run to the phone, I get there in time. I push a button and I see on the screen: "Call over" I am cursed. I look at the instruction book and confirm that it is the right button. What is going on? Nevertheless I heard your message and that appeased me. I am content.

August 26

What I began to feel two days ago is now a fact. The Anna effect has little by little yielded to the depression of a while ago. It is obviously the proof that I need you beside me.

August 27

It was good to hear your voice on the answering machine. It was even very good to hear you. The veil of sadness lifted yesterday at the end of the day. My friends are starting to return. We were six at dinner. That gave me something to do and helped chase away my sorrows. If only life was as simple as cooking. Now there are fewer than 150 hours. The act of counting them helps me put up with your absence. I had the great pleasure of receiving two letters this morning. They help to warm me a bit more. Still I need cold showers to settle me down. Arthur Miller, despite *Death of a Salesman,* never seemed to me to be a New York Jew. He always appeared to me to be bigger and more universal than his origins would predict. For me he remains among the handful of courageous people during the McCarthy period.

August 28
Five days to go. Come quickly my love.

August 29
Your voice; your message received at 6:30. What a pleasure! How I miss you! A good day despite your absence. For company, I had only Eric Orsenna's, *Grand amour.* It was not you but it made for good company anyway. I laughed out loud several times which earn me distrustful looks and hostile glances. The hell with them! He is fantastic!

August 30
I think it is very good that we act like teenagers. There is no reason to let youngsters have all the thrills. The surge of desire is better appreciated and savored in the ripeness of age. What counts for us is quality.

August 31
I think it is hilarious that you do not lose an opportunity to repeat to me that we have a date on September 2, at 12:30. As if I could forget! Be reassured, my love, your charms are such that I am sure to remember.

September 1
Wow! Two letters! I am beginning to get ready for tomorrow. A short run. Lots of fantasy. It is curious how I got used to our separation. Another example of the fact that I adjust to the situation. Yes, you exist, but you are also ephemeral. During long periods of my life I was forced to adjust. Did I succeed? Do I have a gift? I adjusted to being

separate but I also found peace and security during our brief time together. It is these two feelings that have stayed with me during these last three weeks. I missed you; sometimes very acutely; above all physically. Yet at the same time the fact that we found one another, that we shared moments together, that we made love, eased my despair and sadness that so often blew over me these last years. These feelings of mourning, loss, and sadness have moved a bit from their hold on my spirit. They are still there but they are less, decidedly less, painful than before. And in the foreground there are my thoughts about you.

September 2
Finally! William's day! Like a child on Christmas Day I got up at 4:23. Alas, no gifts to open. I note that on my date book I have written "12:30 PM. Hurry up!" I will try, my love. But I hope I will not be too rushed.

Like two youngsters we fall into each other's arms. Heady evenings, greedy hands, wet kisses mark the time. Since we are adults however, we establish a daily rhythm, lived at a lively pace. We alternate museums and art exhibits with movies, dinner at my place or his, books are exchanged, music listened to together; all is sweet. William wishes to show me off to his friends, I am in a hurry to have him meet my children. We are busy with one another. For two months I awake every morning thinking I will see him tomorrow or the day after. It is perhaps the same for him.

Our knowledge of each other deepens. There are stories of the past and photographs. I look at a young boy in short pants on a Bronx street. There is his mother a beautiful Russian with deep eyes. A smiling energetic father. Both dead. For 50 months he went daily to make dinner for his bed ridden mother and administered her medications and injections. More than four years! What filial devotion and unending dedication. One evening while going to her home he was hit by a car. Broken bones, concussion, and assorted injuries. He awakes in a Hospital and his first thought is of his mother; his wife had taken care of her in his absence.

And of course he speaks to me about her. Joy his never ending love. Forty-five years of faithful love. The photos show a thin small figure with dark short hair and a lovely serious look. A medical secretary, she works all her life before being struck by the cancer that ravaged her lungs. He cared for her for five years. The last year, he washed her and changed her. The body so long and so much loved he cherished like that of a child, he bathed her and tucked her in bed. The experience is impossible to communicate to another. When I ask him if in the last year he did not desire a woman, he shakes his head no with a stricken look.

But these sad moments are brief. The rule is William's good humor and his smile - an unshakable smile. There are also his theatrical gestures and his big hugs when we meet. His good byes are also a bit too much. His joy is contagious. I surprise myself by imitating these gestures and greetings. Our pleasure in being together is so large that we do not contain ourselves in public. We do not kiss but we remain always in contact with one another. My arm around his waist, his on my shoulders. I never see disapproving looks or resentful glances. Paris is a huge welcoming city. We go our way among the crowd, anonymous and happy.

Gatherings among friends are marked by well-watered evenings. It is in these moments that I realize the important place that wine holds for William. It was already signaled by his way of decorating his dining room. His tipsiness happily only accentuates William's good humor. As one bottle is replaced by another, William's laughter becomes louder and more jolly. Yet behind this good nature there is a critical intelligence. The wine must be good. When it is not up to standard, it remains in the glass. He looks only for wines of quality that he buys sometimes at the vineyard, sometimes at wine fairs, other times at auction. The prospect of a wine tasting is heaven for him. He cancels all his appointments so as to be present. His meetings with growers are sacred moments, they are special and unique. He goes to the vineyards or to fairs most of the time alone. He buys for friends. He looks over the future of nearly a dozen cellars that he refills according to the needs of his friends. Bordeaux,

Burgundy, Beaujolais, the wines of the Loire Valley are all familiar to this American. He is able to identify them in blind tastings. He looks for less known wines. He is well known by the growers; they appreciate him and pamper him.

And suddenly I realize the significance of my memory loss last year when I had forgotten the name of the Rue Vavin. There is the word "vin" in the street name (Vin in French is wine in English). That wine I so distrusted, that wine that my grandfather drank and which made him drunk every evening. I was ten years old and after dinner I listened to him every night when he went to his room which was next to mine. He bumped into the furniture all the while cursing. Every evening the same drunken display. It was the wine associated with that memory that I wished to forget. The recollection of those moments came back to me but now I was more forgiving. I will continue to be wary of wine and I think that is wise. I wish to be a chaperone, a benevolent watch person. It is a role that is fitting for me and does not cause me too worry. A bit later William will make up for me a selection of inexpensive wines and I will for the first time in my life have a wine cellar.

What makes for his renown among his friends even more that his wine expertise is his culinary skill. Like a real chef he serves his guests individual plates prepared and decorated in the kitchen. Sometimes there are American dishes, such as spare ribs marinated and roasted in the oven, or a marvelous, smooth cheese cake. There is also French cooking based on traditional recipes like hence the association potatoes with sorrel or quail with oyster mushrooms. What he really likes to cook are poultry dishes with cream. A rich, unctuous ivory colored cream that he buys by the ladle from his friend at the cheese store. Calmly and quietly with great concentration he creates a meal for eight or twelve from the opening course through desert. By some miracle the twelve plates come to the table very warm, all prepared and served at the same time. It is a display of Art. The meal goes on; the glasses are merrily filled. The only off note is the sound of the kitchen alarm indicating to the master that a cooking time has been reached. He is unruffled as he manipulates his copper pots, serves his garnishes, and bastes his dishes. I, who panic when I have to serve more than two people, admire his coolness. It is a talent that he inherited from his mother, who was an excellent cook, that was supplemented by his useful experience as a waiter and cook so as to help pay for his education, and a long history of eating in starred restaurants.

When October arrives we decide to enjoy autumn in Normandy. We look over the bends of the Seine from the heights of the Chateau Gaillard, which is deserted at this time of year. Then it is on to the great cathedral in Rouen; followed by the Abbey aux Hommes and aux Dames in Caen. There is the lovely little Fine Arts Museum in Honfleur where we will rediscover the works of Eugène Boudin, so fine and touched by a delicate veil of mist. In the evening we are in the restaurant, sitting in front of a giant seafood platter, with our eyes shining with delight.

I glance around me and seeing that no one is looking, I slip off my shoe and slide my foot between William's legs. He gasps.

- "Foxy Lady," he says with a smile.

I learn that this is a term in American English for an enticing, inviting female. Foxy comes from the word fox, I find in the dictionary. This means crafty, cunning and shrewd. I am good for Foxy Lady; the expression is close enough to sexy to please me. I will adopt it as my own. These are moments of laughter and joy before the catastrophe.

After dinner we walk on the beach at water's edge in total darkness, our arms around each other. The gentle sound of the breaking waves keeps us from entering the black water.

Illness did not enter our castle on tiptoes; it came storming in breaking all the windows and breaching all the doors. Our tiny eight weeks of delight became mere memories and our existence a series of worries. Cancer came in with a rush. It demanded an immediate surgical reaction - the removal of a kidney. The prostate will perhaps be next. The American Hospital in Neuilly became the center of activity. The days just before the operation are hectic and sad. There is no available room. The Hospital is full but the operation cannot be put off. I am not able to conceive that William's life is threatened. We have no plan, everything is on hold. The operation begins at 11AM. That evening I telephone the Hospital and am told that William is doing fine. He was awake for a while and has now gone to sleep for the night. The party at the other end of the line is helpful. I imagine my partner in the recovery room sleeping like a baby under a dim light. The next day I learn that the diseased kidney was well "encapsulated," there is therefore no risk of metastasis. I am relieved. I enter the recovery area after being questioned at the reception desk. William is lying on a trolley in the center of a window less room furnished with many machines and screens. It looks like a laboratory. There is a large glass observation opening which allows him to be watched all the time. He looks like a harpooned lobster.

- "I am a homeless person," he says to me with a laugh.

There is no available room and he will have to stay three more days in this recovery room. He sports a short sleeved hospital gown and features an oxygen tube in his nose. However, his cheerfulness reassures me. I brought for him the latest number of the *Cuisine et Vins de France*. He is enthusiastic about the photographs. The issue is mainly concerned with New Years Eve dinner. We keep distant the fact of illness despite the morphine pump that he uses from time to time whenever he begins to feel pain. Every usage is announced by the ringing of a bell.

During his time in Hospital, I enter into an unexpected intimacy with him. I am there when his dressings are changed and his sessions with the bed pan. His urologist talks to me as if I was part of William's family. These are small compensations for our forced separation. His friends are frequent visitors. Some I already have met. I realize the extent of his many friendships.

Once he is discharged there is the need for a prostate biopsy which will determine if there is a second cancer in this strange gland whose position in the body is unknown to me. If he requires an operation, William has a seventy percent chance of being impotent and a five percent chance of being incontinent. He refuses to accept such odds and prefers a hormonal treatment before radiation therapy which is less risky although longer. Such a treatment however utterly destroys sexual functioning because of the suppression of testosterone production. I ask myself for how long? Will it be a few months? Several years? I weakly protest. The choice will be William's. The verdict is delivered a few days later. The biopsy is positive. The question now is has this second cancer metastasized to his bones? There are more Hospital appointments: A skeletal scan followed by a bone scan. The latter reveals an acute osteoporosis. William is exhausted. He has not lost his smile but he is worried. He is haunted by the idea that there is already a third cancer somewhere and that it will do him in. I try my best to reassure him. The proverbial "never two without three" is this time wrong. There are no lesions on the bone. However all this costs a fortune. As part of his retirement package as a History Professor from the City University of New York he has medical insurance. For a moment he has to leave a blank signed credit card slip at the Hospital. Finally, the insurance for his Hospital stay arrives and he is relieved.

William has faith in his doctors but his sleep is disturbed. The hormonal treatment gives him hot flashes. He has to shed some clothes when this happens and then put them back on when he has shivers. These hot flashes and cold attacks occur several times an hour. They awaken him during the night and prevent him from falling back to sleep. The treatment is supposed to go on for six months. The last two will be accompanied by radiation therapy. He will have to go to the Hospital during June and July five times a week. He tells me all this with a smile. I think about those Jews who speak with laughter of their time in the concentration camps. Is it optimism or recklessness? I do not find this amusing at all. We have not made love for months and no one knows when we will be able to renew our union. In addition, William avoids all physical contact with me. Since his operation he no longer touches me. He has withdrawn from the world and taken his distance from me. The words of love are no longer part of his vocabulary. One day he informs me that I must find another partner as he is no longer available. I protest, I refuse, I am despairing. I no longer even dare to hold his hand. His face is empty of feeling. We kiss on the cheek like old friends. One day he explains to me that since he has fallen ill he has witnessed the return, one after another, of all his subjects of sadness. His sorrow over the death of Joy is stronger than ever. He thinks of her constantly and these memories cause him to suffer. Our time together had pushed back these sad thoughts. He believed that he loved me. He sees now that this is not the case. No love of the moment is strong enough to counter his forty-five years of happiness.

Stubbornly, I stick by him. Some friends encourage me. They tell me that sick people have strange thoughts. I am determined not to let die this just born love. I hope that when I will be again in his arms he will offer me tenderness. That is all I expect - some tenderness. The weeks go by, the sadness stays. One afternoon after a lunch together I try to lead William to my bedroom for a nap. I must put my arms around him. He tears himself away from me. He says I make him face his impotency. He grabs his jacket and leaves without another word. I am struck by the force of this rupture. I cry so much that I develop an enormous fever blister on my bottom lip. My face is a mess. Angry and upset, I decide to place another ad in *Fusac*. The same ad that worked so well the first time. I send William a note telling him what I intend to do. He agrees with me. He has a distant demeanor which I do not like. It is as if he is already dead. The ad comes out. When I see it in black and white I make a complete about face. The blond who is described is not me. It could not be me. I am William's. I can only be his. I am ready to wait for him. I will wait for him till my dying day if I must. The ad is supposed to run a second time. I call the review and cancel it. Then I call my soul mate. I want to see him. He agrees to meet me and I fly toward him. The barrier breached, I hold his hands; he protests feebly. He does not protest long. I clutch his hands to my chest; I do not dare to put my arms around him. I assure him that everything will work out. What we are living through now is a test. It will make us stronger. He will rediscover all his powers in a few months. I am sure of this. He does not contradict me. We take leave of each other with these promises. There is uncertainty present but my courage is restored. I now know what I must do. I must win again William's love - one step at a time. I need to reconquer his affection since there is only that to gain. Limited though this ambition is, it will be enough. It will help me live through the coming months.

New Year's Eve reinforces my determination. Forgetting his cancer, William is cooking for Lou, an old friend living in Florida, for Rafa and Isa as well as a Spanish family visiting them. In a huge pizza or paella pan, he lightly sautes 28 slices of fresh foie gras that he serves with sliced mango. This is followed by fourteen plates of roasted wild boar accompanied by a red cabbage dish, the recipe for which he found at the Pompidou Center Library. At midnight we honor the Spanish tradition and eat twelve grapes at the stroke of twelve. At two o'clock in the morning William sings with Lou and Rafa a *New York, New York* full of feeling and joy. An hour later he escorts me home with a firm hand. We have not kissed, but he let me, in front of his friends, place for a good while my hand on his thigh - a gesture of ownership and intimacy.

Extracts from Anna's Diary

January 31st

William kissed me for the first time in three months. A virginal kiss. I told him "I am happy." "Why?" "Because you love me...." "There you go again....Have you not learned anything? "

February 3rd

He gave me a present of George Gershwin's *An American in Paris.* It was listening to this music when he was a youngster that he fell in love with Paris. I type the title on the Net and get a biography. Gershwin had a unstable childhood growing up in the poor neighborhoods of New York. The son of a Jewish family with Russian roots, like William, he was not able to study music at school. Little George was brought up in the street. In 1904, after listening to the *Melody in F* of Anton Rubinstein, he finds his calling. He plays on the piano of his brother. His time in business school is a waste. He begins to work as a "song plugger" repeating on the piano the latest hits so as to encourage buyers. He meets Fred Astaire. He begins composing. He is barely twenty when his songs begin to be well known. In 1927 he has a success with *Funny Face,* starring Fred Astaire. He travels in Europe. He asks Prokofiev and Ravel for lessons. To continue in Europe is to be condemned to poverty. He refuses this. Yet it is in Paris, in his room at the Majestic Hotel that he is inspired to create the music for a ballet that takes the form of the rhapsody *An American in Paris*. It will be played for the first time during a concert at Carnegie Hall on December 13, 1928.

As he explains, "My objective is to reproduce the impressions of an American tourist when he wonders in this city and hears all the street noises and is replete with the atmosphere of France. "

In the evening when I am depressed, I play this so gay and so happy music.

February 10th

Dinner with American friends, Lorna and Patrick. William has us taste a brandy made from walnuts. I cite a line from a movie, "You have to admit that it is a drink for a real man" William's response, "then it is not for me. I am no longer a man."

We see each other only once a week. Is this a sign of maturity or of separation? I opt for the former because we have "to hold out" until late September.

February 14th

I ask him why he is so nonchalant when discussing his cancer. His reply "because I do not really want to live."

February 19th

After dinner at the Indian restaurant, I pull him towards me." Bitch! "he cries out while smiling and waving good bye. The word must not have the same sense for each of us. I should discuss with him *That's Why the Lady is a Tramp*.

February 21st

I also have bit by bit changed my vocabulary. I no longer dare use the words "my love." Before him, no one had ever called me that. I guess, it was too common a phrase. One day I had enough and I angrily sent him a letter with "my love, my love, my love… "arranged in six columns of twelve lines each.

March 2nd
William welcomed in his house for five days his closest New York friends, Robert and Terry and their daughter, a University student in Montreal. It was a too rare pleasure for me to speak English. Robert talks about Bush and Guantanamo and the violations of Human Rights. He compares Bush to Pinochet. William is unconvinced, "You mean he is a dictator? "He cries. I agree completely with Robert. Bush should be, one day, judged on this affair.

Once his friends have left, William talks to me about his loneliness.

March 5th
In the movies, William lets me hold his hand. He grabs mine in return and feverishly strokes it for the entire film.

I find a book at the Pompidou Center Library, *Les vieux, ça ne devrait jamais devenir vieux*
**Translator's note: Old People Should Never Become Old.* by Pierre Sansot. Not a word about sex. At the library, I speculate how many users are engaged in some form of masturbation. That one over there continually smoothes a curl in her hair; another strokes her chest, a hand slipping into the V opening of her blouse.

March 11th
Every time I go to see William I wear a raspberry colored panty that he likes very much. I do this even though I know he will not see it. He told me that he bought some

underwear. He has one pair in pink that he wore mischievously in the past. He tells me, "I am saving it." I take that to mean it will be used in the future.

March 12th

To surprise, to change continually, to never be the same, to let free imagination each day, to not let routine take over, to not let "the ordinary" take over - such is my wish.

March 14th

It is the anniversary of Joy's death. I call William in the morning. With a lively voice he tells me, "Do you know what I did? I reread all your letters." I was afraid he would be sad and I had thought of things to say.

March 15th

William reveals a secret to me. "Mr. Happy has gone to sleep," and he makes a clear sign with his hand to show me what he means. That evening, I close the curtains, I put on Gershwin's music and I fondle myself with a vibrating "Mr. Happy" made of pink plastic. It is a question of not letting the motor rust away.

March 16th

My evening prayer: "Lord give me strength, courage and patience but not acceptance …."

March 17th

During the program about health on Channel 5, they spoke about the Viagra scams on the Net. 43 % of these pills have no active ingredient.

At my favorite Library I run across the book, *Vivre sans elle (Living without her)* by Groupe Sol, a collection of essays. One is based on thirty some interviews with widowers over 65. The survivor after a period of mourning often does not wish to have sexual relations with another partner. She would become identified not only as a replacement for his longtime partner but above all as a substitute for his beloved. He stays faithful to his other and by doing so is faithful to himself. He wishes not to erase the importance of the time spent together or diminish the memory of former pleasures. The search for pleasure is thus less important than the memory of pleasure. This latter, they do not wish to give up at any price. For many, to begin another relationship is too upsetting because it means over turning all that which was formerly cherished.

Fortunately, William is not made like that. He is rather a willing prisoner of pleasure.

March 21ˢᵗ
Finally, spring is here!
To go to my drawing class at the Ecole des Beaux Arts, I take the Rue du Fg St Denis, go by the Porte de Saint Denis and go down the street so named. I say hello to the prostitutes lounging on their doorstep as I pass. I make a right at the Rue de Rivoli and a left so as to cross the Cour Carrée of the Louvre. I stop on the Footbridge called la Passerelle des Arts and lean for a moment on the railing so as to admire the most beautiful view in Paris. The tourist boats and barges come and go. I finish on the Rue Bonaparte and the display windows featuring books and furnishings. The entire trip took 55 minutes.

March 22ⁿᵈ
I get a letter from William. He writes me that he does not want to live a lie and that he is not in love with me. It is a form of honesty that I could well live without. He wrote that

during a Sunday when he was depressed.

April 1st

April in Paris, why are you so cold?
April in Paris, why are you so sad?

April 5th

William had an appointment with his urologist. His hormonal therapy is extended for another two months and his radiation treatment will not be able to begin before June 15th. He is disappointed; however, nothing has changed. That evening I do not dare call him.

April 6th

William tells me over the telephone the following joke: It concerns an American scientific study of three groups of patients with heart problems. People pray for the well-being of the members of the first group, who do not know that they are so blessed. The second group is prayed for but they are aware of this. The third group receives no prayers at all. The result? The second group is subject to multiple cardiac complications. We laugh.

I tell this story to my son Lucien. He advises me, "all you have to do is pray and say nothing to him."

April 7th

We go together to the Wine Growers Fair at the Espace Champerret. This time I realize that I am in a special place. We taste a flowery and delicious Gewurztraminer. We leave with three bottles and a receipt for an order of Chiroubles and Saint-Amour that William will pick up tomorrow morning with his car. Life still holds for us some splendid days!

During all these months where we are subject to the limitations imposed by illness, there are two activities that bring us together on regular bases and allow us to bear the wait for better days. Our naps together and our visits to museums and galleries are priceless. Not a week goes by without us meeting somewhere so as to admire paintings or photographs. There is Ingres at the Louvre, a Cezanne - Pissarro exhibit at the Orsay Museum, Bonnard at the Musee d'Art Moderne, Magritte at the Maillol, Picasso-Dora Maar at the Hotel Salé, and then Henri Rousseau at the Grand Palais. We hasten together to see all these marvelous events, yet we do so for different reasons. I wish to be touched and moved by the Fine Arts. This has become more and more difficult. All that is needed to destroy the atmosphere and my pleasure is a large group of tourists with their guide. Instantly the visit becomes for me less attractive. It is impossible to have an emotional moment in a room where a holder of a degree in Art History is talking loudly. Biographical details and artistic curiosities are more burdensome than useful to me. I love to fill myself in silence with a masterpiece. Thirty years ago, it was possible. Museums today are too crowded, even in the morning just after their opening. I continue to go to museums so as to enhance my knowledge. William feels the same, but his formal training as a historian makes him more forgiving of the tour guide. When the exhibition is of quality, we leave content. This is almost always the case. Still I am nostalgic for a time where I could go alone, wander from room to room, make a quick about face so as to surprise a painting that was too quickly viewed the first time. I remember so fondly a time when I was able to take in a whole room with a glance and be pulled toward a masterpiece which was familiar to me without regard for dates or waiting for the painting to be clear of human obstruction. Undoubtedly, museums will no longer ever have for me their former charm. Yet they are more attractive for having been visited as a couple. It would not be hard for me to make up a prize list of glorious moments spent together in museums, giving often two stars to those special times.

I would award, however, three stars to the tender naps that we take after our lunches together. Because often we both have troubles sleeping, these siestas are necessary. They are the best moment of the day. Three months ago William had trouble accepting the idea of being in the same bed without making love. He had the feeling that such a situation diminished him. Now, he cooperates in these "cuddles." At first we lay together fully clothed; later we progressively shed our clothes and we settle in each other's arms for an hour or two of affection. I listen to William sleep and hear the funny little noises he makes. He awakens frequently, smiles at me, gives me a hug and goes back to sleep. I think about us. I am comfortable. I kiss his hands. The fourth star will have to wait for the end of the year when we can be still closer. These sessions are not certainly what I would have wished for but they are tender and restful. They allow us to hold out while awaiting better. The warmth of the bed, our innocent kisses, the sweetness of our intertwined bodies make us languid after these moments of happiness, enchantment and love.

However there is one subject that we discuss fairly often which separates us - metaphysics. William is a very unkosher Jew. He is a militant atheist. As a young boy he teased his observant buddies by eating sausages in front of them on Yom Kippur, the most solemn High Holy Day, which requires Jews to fast. Now, he often teases me for my somewhat childish mysticism. I am not a good Christian. I do not believe in the Divinity of Christ and all the oddities surrounding the Holy Mother leave me wondering but not scornful. My relationship with God is personal. I do not need the intercession of a clergy. Nevertheless, I have recently agreed to be the Godmother of Clement in addition to being his grandmother. I am not anticlerical. I believe in the complete separation of Church and State. Yet, I am a passionate believer. I have cried when listening to a Mozart mass and I pray every evening for our American pen pals condemned to death. However, this difference of belief between William and I does not lead to friction. We make concessions to the other and our sense of humor allows us to pass over this conflict.

Today, June 4th, is the Anniversary of the revolt culminating in Tiananmen Square. It was during the night in 1989 that tanks invaded this famous place and bloodily crushed the student uprising. At 2 PM I am on the large esplanade, called the Human Rights Square, of the Trocadero for the annual memorial to mark the event. One hundred odd people have gathered, representing all the groups concerned. Of course, there are many Chinese; some in mourning clothes. One of them hands out yellow roses. Marie Holzman, a noted sinologist, forbidden to set foot in China, who is President of Solidarité Chine, introduces me to M. Xu Wenli, a political prisoner who managed to escape after seventeen years in jail. His face, a study in courage and compassion is very moving to me.

Speaker after speaker talks in Chinese. Their remarks are translated by Caï Chongguo, a philosophy Professor who swam his way to Hong Kong and freedom the night of June 3rd. fortunately he was picked up by a boat and saved. Since that time he lives in France. That is more or less the legend which has been created about him. He is so handsome and so Chinese, with his hair always well groomed and flecked with gray, his proper French seasoned with a light accent; he represents, by his very presence, the incarnation of Chinese resistance.

A collective of different organizations has just been formed with the goal of informing the public about the serious violations of Human Rights in China, where the Olympic Games of 2008 will be held. This supra-organization called China 2008 has determined that the preparations for the Olympics has been marked by an increase of repression in flagrant disregard of the promises made by the Chinese Government.

At the end of their presentation, each speaker pledged to meet, as they have every year for the past seventeen, next year at Tian'anmen Place.

Next year at Tian'anmen Place....

That evening William shows me three small crosses traced in ink. Two are on one side of his pubic area and another at the beginning of his penis. These points will be used to focus the x-ray beams of his radiation treatments, which will begin in less than two weeks. He is ready; he is pleased to begin soon. Each session will last four minutes. During the first week they will be at 6:30 PM. Later, treatments will be at different times; they will extend over eight weeks.

Two days later, the black crosses are replaced by tattoos. During the next forty-eight hours William could not take a bath. A cruel deprivation for someone who had taken the trouble to make a splendid bathroom and order a beautiful tub for his apartment in the Rue du Rocher.

Yet, there is good news; he was able to reduce the hormonal treatment to every other day. From that moment there is a great improvement. We begin again to sleep together and kiss passionately. Our ardor stops there. When I put my hand on the front of William's underwear he sadly says, "you will not find anything hard in my pants." However, little by little, we begin to feel alive once again.

Yesterday I went alone to see the film *The road to Guantanamo* by Michel Winterbottom and Mat Whitecross. It is the story of three young Englishmen of Pakistani descent. Ruhel, Sahfig, and Asif leave an English village in October 2001 to celebrate the wedding of one of the three in a Pakistani village. Once there, they listen to an Imam calling the faithful to aid the Afghan population in difficulty. The three leave for Kaboul. They are picked up during an attack led by soldiers of the Northern Alliance against the Taliban. They are considered sympathizers of Al Qaida and soon thereafter as soldiers of that movement. The film shows their hellish treatment: interrogations, imprisonment in cells so small that only one of them can sleep at a time, then their transfer in cages to Guantanamo. Manacled for hours to a ring in the floor, they are tortured by thundering music and flashing lights. Some prisoners scream for help, others become insane. Part reconstitution, part documentary, the film has the ring of truth. The three will not be tried after two years of prison. They will be released in 2004 without any explanation.

In bed, after dinner, William announces in a sad voice,
- "Anna, you did not make a good choice...."
I have been expecting these moments of discouragement but I am as worried as he is. The next day I will write him a letter. I have made a habit to send him short love letters since I know he saves them and rereads them. One day, referring to these letters, he says to me:
- "You make me happy."
I do not remember exactly when I assured William that even if he did not recover his sexual capacity I would not leave him. Perhaps it was one of those nights that we spent kissing like two children. All of a sudden sex did not seem so important to me. I write to William that everything that we had in common, our tastes, our thirst for knowledge and

culture, all that should be enough for us, and that it would be enough for me. This declaration lightened the tension between us. He answered me that nevertheless he made no promises for the future. It is possible that he would drift away from me. Perhaps he would no longer have the strength to sleep with me. I had the feeling that everything was starting anew. That he was once again ready to retreat to his lair. Once again I would have to be patient and reconquer little by little what I had once won. I snapped. I wrote him that if we could not any longer sleep together, it would be better to split up. He was terribly upset and soon thereafter he had to retract what he had advanced as a possible future. Because of this I realized just how uncertain and fragile we were as a couple.

Despite all the turmoil, after the promise I had made, our relations became more positive. He began again to invite me with his friends and introduce me to them. I began again to make plans for the future. William refuses to consider the idea of living together. His apartment is not set up for that. He does not wish to move and leave familiar surrounding; what he calls his village. At the least I hope to live in his neighborhood, close to him, with his help. He has already financially helped me. I find that reassuring. Our union is becoming official, material considerations will help it last.

Now that we have began again to spend nights together, I look at William in his underwear. I see his pectorals which have become breast-like because of the hormonal treatment to reduce testosterone levels. I see the weight that he has added around his waist. He is always too tired to run as he had. I am afraid that he is continuing to gain weight. Illness has deformed him and made him ponderous. Perhaps this is impossible to change. Yet I feel very tender towards this damaged body.

He speaks to me of the waiting room which he visits

since the beginning of his radiation treatments at the Hartmann Clinic. Every day he is there for 15 to 40 minutes. It is the most painful moment because this wait makes him relieve the awful time when all the treatments imaginable did not save Joy. There are women in the waiting room with their mammographies in their hands and men with the echographs of their prostate. You can easily see fear on their faces; unless this fear is only the reflection of William's own. Last week a totally bald woman waited next to him. Another patient was carried in. More than all the treatments given him, he is most upset by his wait among other cancer patients. The radiation itself is painless. It lasts only a moment. When the technician calls him, he undresses in a tiny cubicle that he calls the "cell." He then lies down on the "machine" and lowers his underwear so as to reveal his tattoo marks. It is the "machine" which moves around him with its whistling noise. Four minutes and its over, yet his life is controlled by his treatments. It is this latter which organizes his day.

Several times I accompany my dear friend in his wait. I saw women with imaginative head pieces. There was a woman wearing a blue straw cloche, another a wide brim spangled hat, both wished to hide their radiation caused baldness. Men are less timid, several show their shaved head. On my left there is a couple seated whose knees are touching. She is holding a large manilla envelope containing the results of some examination. He looks defeated, his shoulders are slumped, his features are drawn. Who is the sick one? A little further there is a man in a wheelchair. An aide brings him a glass of water.

- "It's something to drink!" the old man says with a smile.

- "It is only an ounce, "says the aide with a mock

seriousness.

A heavy woman comes in the room. She is all smiles. On her head she has tight a blue printed handkerchief. She sits down all the while talking with others. This waiting room is a distillation of humanity. In a movie, it would be a quite good parable for the desperation of the human condition.

In his free time in between radiation treatments William wrote a kind of diary where he speaks about me; it is more a series of thoughts and analyses.

Excerpts from William's Notes

July 12th

The verb "to know" is slight, weak, vague and inadequate. It demands an adjective to give it sense. Coupled with hardly, well, or intimately, to know takes on some size and meaning. Yet the uncertainty of the naked, unassisted verb is appropriate when applied to A.

Winston Churchill, speaking of Russia, called the land and its people "a puzzle rapped inside a mystery, hidden in an enigma." A. Is not quite as unfathomable; yet she is far from obvious. What you see is not what you get; what you get is not what you expect; what you expect is at times not forthcoming. In the successive layers of her persona are found part of her charm, a substantial measure of intrigue, enigmas to resolve, mysteries to answer, and puzzles to solve.

Any work of detection is not aided by A. She hides more than she reveals. She is reluctant rather than forthcoming. She obscures rather than clarifies. This alternation of light and shadow is found in her appearance, her memories and her opinions. Is it because she is timid? Modest? Indifferent? Is it an affirmation of great self-confidence? Or a sign of a lack of same?

July 15th

A. is surrounded by questions. Questions which arise even when you try to describe her. Why does a lovely woman make little effort to be more lovely? Why does a deeply sensual woman present herself in a non-sexual manner? Why does someone who does not look her age dress older than she is?

Questions. Questions, without adequate answers. How is it that a supremely intelligent woman has abandoned all reason in the pursuit of love? And why has she done so several times? We are confident that great intelligence does not repeat an error; not the case with A. We are accustomed to the idea that age tempers passion and that moderation replaces recklessness; not true of A.

Why does A. not speak of her creative accomplishments? Is it that she is too modest? Is it that she does not feel the need "to explain" that which she has wrought? In this age of hard sell for all that is "created" she is quite unique. We see and hear everywhere authors, artists, architects, composers –creators of all types – compete for attention in "explaining" that which should be evident. A. is not part of that market cacophony. Why? And what conclusions can we reach from this fact? Is it that A. is animated by a great self-confidence? Is her silence due to timidity? Or to indifference? Perhaps she does not sing her own praises because the creative act is her reasons to be. To write, to sketch, to put brush to canvas is enough for A. It is by these acts that she breathes and lives. Fame and praise do not count for A. The contrast and the questions continue.

July 19th

A. is an activist. A different sort of activist than the overwhelming majority of the comrades. She never speaks of the good she does. She never inflates the value of her activities. She never justifies. She never boasts. She never imposes her opinions and positions on others. She does. She looks for no acclaim. She does. She seeks no applause. She does. Without fanfare, without self-congratulation, she does. She acts to save some people from legal murder; she works to save part of the planet; she works against tyranny and injustice. And the selflessness of this work, and the purity of her motivation, put to shame all but a handful of the world's population. This activism gives rise to another mystery. Why is A. so different from most other activists? Such rare behavior is most often the result of religious fervor. A's idea of God is like those of the 18th Century philosophers. Yet she says she prays. Deists did not believe in an intervening Deity. A. does.

July 22th

A. is often accommodating, flexible, tolerant and adaptable. Often. A. is capable of getting lost because she finds a certain format of a Metro map ugly and thus refuses to look at it. The problem with her dislikes is that she does not reveal them in advance and they do not fall into a coherent pattern. A. is the most attentive of listeners up to the moment when without warning, the turns inward and disappears into a secret place where she alone lives. Question A. about the facts of her life and you receive little information; yet her novels are full of episodes drawn from her life. A. shows little interest in the chronology or dates of her life. Yet she is capable of reliving a feeling of decades ago.

August 4th

The first time I met A. I wanted to protect her. I wanted to assure her that she would be safe with me. I wanted to erase the anxiety and sadness on her face. When I saw her smile, I wished to make that smile permanent. I wished to bask in the warmth of that smile. Yes, it is a completely male chauvinist, macho response, perhaps deserving of contempt but heartfelt nevertheless.

August 9th

This effort "to know" A. is moved by a belief that if I know her I will be certain of what she wants out of our couple. For A. it is very simple. She wants me to love her as she loves me. But we have very different definitions of that four letter word, love. I am not afraid of this word. I say "I love you" almost every day. Sometimes repeatedly. Alas, someone no longer hears these so often said words. I repeat these words before, during and after tears. I say them and mean them as I said and meant so often and for so long. I do not think I will ever be able to say them to another –no matter how cherished she can be. They are all that remains of that monument and glory that was our life during forty five years. I cannot vandalize it.

August 11th

Several times I have told A. "I can only offer what I can offer." My feelings and my actions are circumscribed by how I have lived my life. It is impossible for me to shed my past. To try to do so is to commit moral suicide. In addition I have unanswered questions. Am I really cured? Will I be sexually whole again? Will I be freed from this terrible, all-encompassing fatigue? Will I be able to accept the debilities of old age and its accompanying restrictions? There are yet to be answered questions about A. and myself. Can our relationship survive and prosper continuing as it has been? Does it require changes in the organization of our lives to survive?

At this moment, I feel that I do not have the energy or the will to alter dramatically my life; or to begin a new life. The life I have lived is my anchor. It comforts me. It grounds me. It consoles me. I am supported by what I have lived and what I was. I am saved by the past and I am condemned to live there and prevented by it from searching for something else. It is my salvation. It is my curse.

A. has said that she would not finish *Sex après 60* until she knows how it will turn out. I do not really know what she means by that. But this is like so much that I do not understand about my dear A. So I also will wait and therein lies another question.

During one of our chaste nights together in August, I was startled awake by one of those crying fits which William spoke about. It was like a soft rustle of leaves shaken by the wind. I knew exactly what was happening. I took William in my arms and I rocked him gently until he finally stop crying. We did not say a word.

I no longer remember the day when we began again "to make love" although it was without the acts of penetration and ejaculation. These incomplete intimacies left us unsatisfied but determined to go forward. I sensed each time William becoming more alive. He was taking Cialis. This is a Viagra like product which is less powerful but without the time constraints of the latter. With the Viagra we were obliged to program our time together; an obligation we both found distasteful. William was disappointed but nevertheless he judged our first efforts promising. Repeated failures did not discourage him. Aftcr one of these failures William said:

- "I don't say if but I say when, I will have regained my sexual powers, you are going to get it girl."

One month later, Wednesday September 6th we see realized our hopes. Everything went at top speed. After caressing me for a very short while, William is in position between my legs. I am terribly afraid that once again he will not be able to follow through. However, he enters me easily and quickly ejaculates with a great sigh of joy. He collapses on top of me with little sounds of happiness and fulfillment.

- "I had forgotten how good it is," he exclaims with a little moan of happiness.

Then, shortly after with a certain sheepishness he takes me by the shoulders and makes a solemn promise.

- "I swear to you that in two months I will become again a good lover."

It took him a week.

My birthday was the day following this triumph. We went to the Galeries Lafayette Department Store to buy some lingerie. A bit astounded by it all, we look at the mannequins decked out in lacy finery. Very quickly we find in the Cacharel section delicate triangles printed with Persian themes. While waiting on line we look at a woman wearing a headscarf accompanied by her husband, we assume, holding in their hands a whole line of different nighties, underwear and bras. They probably are buying for their sisters, nieces and cousins back home in Lebanon or in Syria.

The day after this daring adventure we leave for several days in the Loire Valley. Both William and I like this kind of close tourism. We travel back in time and the history of France. There are Chateaux and Monasteries. Azay-Le-Rideau, Langeais, Ussé, Brissac and Fontevraud are there to welcome us. William impresses me with his knowledge of the Valois and Bourbon Dynasties.

Three days in a row after our visits we make love on clean white sheets without the help of a medical prescription. By the third day William had rediscovered his touch and I found again my pleasure.

After these moments of passionate delight we sit at tables in restaurant terraces and feast on eels and wild mushrooms while drinking white wines of the Loire. My right foot traces a path under the table cloth and finds its mark. William laughs like a teenager.

With our return to Paris the ten months of illness are forgotten. Once again we cannot get enough of each other.

We are like youngsters, our hands and our lips always looking for the other. William has an American word for that: Horny. That means sexually excited sexually aroused. It's true, we are horny.

William is pleased to have chosen not to be surgically treated. The longer but less risky alternative has succeeded. His friends find him in good shape. They do not have to ask how he feels; our good health is obvious. Little by little William regains his strength. He does some woodworking, he runs in the morning in the Park Monceau. As for me I move into a studio near him. It is well lit and has a balcony that overlooks a courtyard paved with traditional blocks and graced by a splendid tree. If there is an emergency, we can in a few minutes have a "quicky."
It will be like a honeymoon.

Our friends are a bit jealous to see us so happy and smiling all the time. My children do not pay attention to all this. They are happy for me and do not ask me questions. I like it like this.

The tree that shades my courtyard is a Linden tree. I will soon pick berries for a herb tea. We will slowly sip this brew on my balcony and peacefully await the nightfall.